# Time Traveling Blues in the City of the Watcher

*Volume Two of the
City of the Watcher trilogy*

**Andrew M. Reichart**

**Weird Books for Weird People**

Also by Andrew M. Reichart from Argawarga Press:

*Wallflower Assassin*

*Weird Luck in the City of the Watcher*

*Cannibal-King*

Argawarga Press is an imprint of Autonomous Press that publishes strange fantasy, horror, and science fiction.

Autonomous Press is an independent publisher focusing on works about neurodivergence, queerness, and the various ways they can intersect with each other and with other aspects of identity and lived experience. We are a partnership including writers, poets, artists, musicians, community scholars, and professors. Each partner takes on a share of the work of managing the press and production, and all of our workers are co-owners.

Front Cover by Mike Bennewitz @sonofwitz

Interior by Casandra Johns



Originally published in 2012 by Argawarga Press

ISBN-13: 978-1-945955-34-1

Argawarga Press • argawarga.com

# Contents

for Sami

# Prologue at the End of Washington, D.C.

Professor Clark shut the door behind him. The air in this reality felt muggy. Agent Xax sat at the foot of the bed, sleeves rolled up, tie loosened, with a cigarette in one hand and a remote control in the other. Clark assessed the room. The peeling wallpaper, thin carpet, and mass-produced furniture suggested an Earth motel room, or perhaps a furnished studio apartment. A hulking television, mounted inside a huge cabinet with chipped veneer, displayed a professional sporting event; Clark quickly recognized it as Australian Rules football.

"So." He straightened the lapels of his ill-fitting suit jacket. "Earth, late Twentieth Century. After the invention of those slim black remotes," he pointed at the device in Agent Xax's hand, "yet before the invention of the slim screen. Impossible to say which decade, exactly, until we know which Earth." He put his hands in his jacket pockets.

"X00023," said Agent Xax. "It's Earth-X00023. Nineteen ninety-eight."

"You deprive an old man one of his few remaining pleasures. I would like to have at least had the chance to guess." Clark nodded toward the television. "Not that I would have guessed that one. Technologically, X-three-oh-twenty-three is decades ahead of most Earths. Why, then, the overlarge television set?"

"It's a lousy hotel, that's why." Agent Xax wiped his brow. "Were you followed?"

"I should hope not!" Clark turned back toward the door. A metal disc shimmered at each corner of the doorway: three small, one larger. Clark reached for one of them, and a racket of explosions erupted in the street outside. He fell into a crouch, joints cracking, and covered his head. Agent Xax didn't move. Clark looked up at him.

"Firecrackers," said Agent Xax. "Fourth of July." He gestured toward the open window, where dawn light had begun fading the night sky to gray. "Fifth, technically." He flicked his cigarette ash on the carpet as punctuation.

"Ah." Clark pushed himself up, annoyed and embarrassed. He began removing the discs from the corners of the doorway. "Sorry I'm late, then."

"I was beginning to wonder if I gave you wrong time differentials for your gate gizmo."

Clark slipped the small discs into a slot on the side of the large one, then put it in his pocket. "I was severely delayed by Woad. How late am I?"

"Never mind. Tell me this. Are you sure you want to replace Woad?"

"You're joking! I should be Acting Archivist, not that buffoon. He isn't even published." He grimaced. "I think he's barely literate."

"Let me ask you this, though. How do you expect to get the keys to the Archive?"

Clark smiled. "The Archivist shares my point of view. He has promised me the keys if I can shut Woad out of the Archive."

Agent Xax furrowed his brow. "What do you mean, 'the Archivist'?"

"I mean the true Archivist, the Great God Thoth." Clark nearly purred.

Agent Xax furrowed his brow. "You're telling me He come out of His coma?"

Clark smiled and nodded. "Nay, He remains petrified ever since the Archive first went interdimensional. The 'Great Breach' as the ensuing Cataclysm was known in that world. But I have divined a way to communicate with Him."

Agent Xax drew on his cigarette, eyeing Prof. Clark. "I'm impressed."

Clark bowed slightly. "We have many resources in the Archive." He frowned. "That oaf Woad only ever obtained the keys to the Archive in the first place because of his Weird Luck."

"I'd have to agree with you." Agent Xax stood. "Well, enjoy the fact that 'weird' doesn't always mean 'good.'" He dropped the remote onto the bed and grabbed his jacket. "Not today, for example. Come on, let's get your new gear and get out of here." He took a last drag of his cigarette and tossed it onto the bed as well before heading for the door.

"Xax," said Clark.

"Come on, we can talk on the way."

Clark pointed at the bed. "That can't be in accord with Reality Patrol regulations." A thread of smoke rose from the smoldering synthetic blanket.

Agent Xax growled dismissively and grabbed the doorknob. "It won't even be here in an hour."

"Precisely my point! The room will likely be gone, perhaps the whole building!"

"No. Clark. None of this is going to be here."

"None of what?"

"D.C.," said Agent Xax. "Come on."

Clark stiffened. "Speak plainly, not in your damn Reality Patrol acronyms."

"Washington, D.C." Agent Xax pointed at the window. "Won't be here. In an hour or so. Happy X-Day: Seven Five Ninety-eight is dawning, so get the lead out." He opened the door.

"Wait." Clark pulled the gate device out of his jacket pocket and brandished it at Xax. He spoke through clenched teeth. "You had me meet you on a notoriously cataclysmic Earth, an hour before their local Cataclysm?"

Agent Xax sighed. "This is the time and place where our contact is meeting us. The person who is going to make you Acting Archivist." Switching to a low growl: "So since time is short, as we know, please come now, before the nukes start flying."

Clark tugged the chain and looked at his watch, put it and the gate back in their respective pockets, and nodded stiffly.

Agent Xax led Clark down an empty hallway to an empty elevator, where he pressed the button for the top floor: Six. The elevator shuddered upward. Jerked to a stop. After an overlong moment the doors parted and Clark followed Agent Xax down another empty hallway, to Room 664. Agent Xax stood to the side of the door, rapidly knocking on it three times, then once, then twice. "Come in," called a loud voice from inside. Agent Xax gestured for Clark to enter. Clark frowned at him for a moment, then opened the door.

On the bed sat two women, one in a corset, one in a bikini, flanking a boyish-faced man wearing a silk bathrobe and a backwards baseball cap. "Clark! Yeah! It *is* you!" He pumped both fists in the air and then pointed at Clark with both hands. "I knew it would be you! Xax wouldn't tell me but I was sure you were the guy."

Clark frowned. "Chester."

"The one and only. And I'm at work, you see." He put his arms around the women beside him. "Furthering the cause of our sacred Archive."

Clark winced. "Furthering the decline, you mean."

"As if, bro. I'm the most popular thing our Order has ever produced and you know it."

"Quantity does not imply quality."

"You pompous shmompous schmuck, I don't just mean my offworld sales. Which are huge, by the way."

Clark sneered.

"You can't argue, dude, pretty much everyone in the Order is a paid subscriber—including you, you hypocrite!"

"I never!" Clark reddened.

"You don't think I know who's watching? I know you were one of my first, dumbass, you can't hide from me just by signing up through a proxy and whatnot."

Clark reddened deeper.

"Sometimes I even watch you baa-aack." Chester winked.

"Impossible!" said Clark, nonetheless visibly uncertain.

"Are you boys cast or crew?" asked the woman in the corset, looking disapprovingly at Clark and Agent Xax.

"Neither, ladies." Chester disengaged his arms to gesture in the air. "Judy, Trudy, this is Agent Xax and Professor Clark."

"Don't call me Judy, it's Judith," said the woman in the bikini.

"But I like the rhyme."

"I don't," said Judith.

"Makes us sound like a pair of trained pets, Chester," said Trudy.

"Okay fair enough, Judith, Trudy, these gentlemen and I have some other business to attend to for a moment, if you don't mind."

"Cutting it a bit close, no?" asked Judith.

"We're good," said Chester, "don't worry, I got my eye on the clock. None of us are gettin' incinerated, not today anyways."

Judith and Trudy strode across the room to the mini-fridge.

"Let's make this quick, eh, Professor?" Chester waggled his eyebrows, causing his cap to waggle in strange counterpoint.

"The quicker the better," said Clark.

Agent Xax closed the door. "I have your document." He held out a dog-eared, inch-thick manuscript clamped at one corner with a binder clip.

"Hey hey hey where'd you have that hidden, chief, hmmm?"

Agent Xax stood, holding the manuscript, unsmiling.

"Just drop it there." Chester pointed with his chin at the desk by the door.

Agent Xax flung the manuscript on the desk. "So." He adopted an exaggerated formality. *"Thank you for bringing this suspicious material to the attention of the Reality Patrol. In exchange for the valuable assistance you have given us, I am pleased to offer you amnesty for past infractions, under the terms we discussed earlier. I also hereby return your confiscated property,"* pulling a metal disc from his pocket and laying it on top of the manuscript. *"During the research process, our analysts programmed your device with the coordinates described in the document, as well as codes to bypass the destination-world's Astral Web. This information is, of course, for your organization's record-keeping purposes only; any actual use of the device for transport to the world identified in the document would be regarded as a severe infraction of interdimensional trespass code, and would be punished accordingly."* He looked at Clark.

Clark narrowed his eyes. "What are you gentlemen talking about?"

Chester bounced up and down on the bed a little. "Don't you love this shit, Clark? I freakin' love this shit." Turning to Agent Xax, he woodenly recited, *"Has the Reality Patrol issued any uh limitation upon my uh transfer of the device?"*

Agent Xax looked back at Chester. *"No prohibition has been specified against your transfer of the device."*

"What the hell are you guys talking about?" asked Trudy.

"Hang on, this is the best part, I'll recap later. Clark, you getting this?"

Clark shook his head brusquely.

Chester stage-whispered, gesturing at the desk. *"Take. The Thing."*

"Just the gate gizmo, not the manuscript," said Agent Xax.

Clark picked up the metal disc, and turned the manu-script so he could read the title page:

*City of the Watcher*
by Aleck Woad

"Am I reading this correctly? An actual Woad text?"

Agent Xax pressed his fingertips down on the manu-script. "You can have the document for your Archive after you do the job."

Clark looked at Chester. "What is *City of the Watcher?*"

"A little something I found somewheres," said Chester.

"Put the gate in your pocket," said Agent Xax. "A different pocket from your gate home."

"I know how to avoid mixing up gates," snapped Clark, slipping the gate into his second gate-pocket.

"Go home," continued Agent Xax. "Lead Woad through the gate you just received from Chester, close the gate be-hind him, and I will escort him out of your way forever."

"No killing." Clark pointed an authoritative finger at Agent Xax.

"I am not an assassin," said Agent Xax.

"Are you Reality Patrol?" asked Judith. "Is this some kind of sting operation?"

"Nah dude," said Chester, "you're gonna love it, I'll tell you in a minute. And then we'd better get to work, so we can get outta here on cue. Whoo-hoo!"

Clark observed Chester's colleagues. Trudy said to Judith, "Even if they were pigs, they've got nothing on us anyway."

"You can beat the rap, but you can't beat the ride," said Judith.

"True, but still," said Trudy, "look at 'em. Whatever this is, it's between those boys and isn't about us."

Their composure made Clark feel even more agitated, which he resented. He redirected his attention to Chester, a source of infinitely more resentment. "Chester, it frankly poisons me that my attainment of leadership of our Order should be tainted by your participation."

"Dude, shut up." Chester pointed at himself with both thumbs. "I'm the best thing ever happened in the history of the Order. You can make up whatever elitist sour grape stories you want, but you can't argue with my numbers." He stood up, making shooing motions. "We have a sex movie to make. Take your gizmo and get out of here, man. You piss me off."

"You don't have to be mean to the old guy," said Trudy.

"Dude, you're defending *that* guy? He thinks what we're doing here isn't even art!"

Judith laughed. "Art?"

"What? It's awesome! We vanish right before the blast hits us, guaranteed viral."

"It's still not Palme d'Or material," said Trudy. "It's just disaster porn. It's not even that rare anymore. I did a job in a force field in a volcano."

"Yeah last year I did a group scene aboard a starship under attack. Still have a shrapnel scar." Judith pulled her hair aside to show Trudy. "Exploding instrument panel."

"Let's get out of here," Agent Xax said to Clark, opening the door and stepping through. "I can't stand these people."

"With pleasure," said Clark.

"Where are the cameras?" asked Judith.

"In my skull!" Chester grabbed his head in both hands.

Clark slid the manuscript into a subdimensional pocket inside his jacket, unseen by anyone, and followed Agent Xax into the hallway.

# The Acting Archivist

Professor Alexander "Aleck" Woad opened the door and peered in. The refrigerator nearly overflowed with food: vegetables from a dozen worlds, innumerable jars of sauces, rare beers, cooked meats, a dozen varieties of cheese. He extricated a flat box and flipped it open to reveal half a cold pizza. He dropped the box on the counter, took a slice, and roamed around the room. His untied boot-laces clicked delicately on bare stone, then skittered even more faintly across the rug.

Aleck's favorite artifacts often found their way into his "smoking room," deep in the Archive of Thoth. He wandered, chewing, between his Earth-X00023 shelf (mostly items salvaged from Oakland, California in the generations after the Big One) and a bookcase of paperbacks from various Earths (science fiction and fantasy novellas from the 1960s and 70s). He found himself facing a shoulder-high section of crumbling stone wall, eight feet wide. The wall came from a world known by several names: Kaios-A00013,

Akazland, Anachronia. Through the center of the wall ran a fist-sized hole. He and various comrades from the Order had transported the wall to the Archive for preservation, years ago. His thoughts, as they typically did whenever he looked at it, ran through his ongoing argument with Professor Clark.

"You have ransacked Kaios-A00013 of one of its precious artifacts," said the imaginary Clark. "The wall at which the monk Athan stared for nine years, drilling a hole through it with the force of his will. You have looted the people of A13 of an irreplaceable cultural relic and hidden it away in your private study, where not even our Order can benefit from it."

"Yeah but dude." In these imagined debates Aleck often found himself woefully inarticulate. "In *every* parallel, the Idiranians frickin' *vaporize* this wall. Fact. And B), this room isn't private, there isn't even a lock on the door, everyone in the Order knows they can come in whether I'm here or not, dammit. It's just a sub-collection like we have in a hundred other rooms."

The imaginary Clark persevered, unfazed, as usual. "Your interference deprived the local folk of the chance to defend it for themselves."

"The frickin' Reality Patrol was backing the Idiranians!" Aleck's voice cracked. "Nothing native to that world could have stopped them—it took Doomer and the whole crew of the *Ace of Shadows* to extricate the wall intact. The Patrol could have nuked the whole Plateau of Leng if they wanted to!"

"Preposterous. The Reality Patrol has never done any such thing, outside of conspiracy theories."

"You seriously believe that," said Aleck.

"Dude dude dude Clark, man," came a new voice, "you should do like Reality Patrol marketing or P.R. or whatever." An imagined Chester Now had appeared out of nowhere, uninvited, as the real Chester Now so often did. Being defended by Chester made Aleck feel all the more illegitimate. A hole somewhere deep in his self-esteem kept him at a permanent disadvantage, apparently, even in the private realm of his own daydreams.

"ACAB," Chester concluded, gesturing with both hands.

"The Archive isn't the goddamn British Museum," Aleck said. "The Order didn't loot the Wall from a people we subjugated. We saved it, and we're going to return it to the folks of A13 as soon as we find sometime safe from the Idiranians, like I said in my report. You want to take the reins of that project, be my guest, heck take the wall with you now if you like."

What bothered Aleck most about Clark's style of argument was his pointing. Whenever a debate got heated, he would jab with his finger: toward the sky, toward the ground, at any physical objects under discussion, or, worst of all, at his opponent. Opponents, rather; Clark started with one (often Aleck), but always swiftly enlisted others to his enemy's side, whatever their opinions, with his excessive antagonism. Aleck's imagined arguments with Clark always ended with Clark's finger stabbing the air an inch from his chest. "Our Order will be exterminated by the Reality Patrol if we continue our frivolous attitude toward interdimensional interference."

*Gesticulating like a little dictator,* Aleck thought to himself, though he couldn't bring himself to say it aloud, not even in his daydream. "We're protected by the Archive," was his only reply. As ever, though, he wondered how true that was, and he wondered if Clark could sense this hole in his conviction.

His daydream evaporated. Aleck found himself staring through the hole in the Wall of Athan. *The Reality Patrol has never been able to find the Archive*, he reassured himself. *The gates in and out of it are impossible to crack, by decree of the Archivist.*

"How did I ever become the frickin' Acting Archivist."

He wandered around the room, finishing his cold slice of pizza, gaze skimming over his shelves of books, musical recordings, trinkets, and talismans. He came face to face with a dusty old mirror. Without the shock of white hair, crow's feet, and laugh lines, he thought he could perhaps pass for thirty. But the sunburst of scars crossing half his face made it hard to judge. How old was he really? "You look like you've seen a lot, buddy." *How did I ever become Acting Archivist?*

"I found the Five Keys to the Archive. That's how." *Five Keys to the Archive*, he thought. *Five Keys to the Archive. Good gravy, I can't even remember what they are, much less where.* He looked around wildly. "The first one is that chrome number five," he remembered: he had found it lying amid broken glass beside a wrecked car. He scanned the room and spotted the Chrome Five immediately, sitting on an old stump, propped against a small idol of Ganesha. He picked it up and scrutinized it.

"What do you have there?" came Clark's real live voice from behind him. Startled, Aleck spun in place, adrenaline coursing painfully into his fingers and toes. "From your birthday cake, age five?"

"This is one of the Keys to the Archive," Aleck said, immediately wishing he hadn't. He quickly put the Chrome Five into his jeans pocket.

"From the auto accident that catalyzed your interdimensional travel powers," said Prof. Clark. "Yes?"

Aleck groaned. "I don't have any interdimensional travel powers. I have a knack for finding gates, that's all." Even as the words came out of his mouth, he knew he would regret Clark's inevitable lengthy reply.

"You create these gates. Admit it. At the very least, your presence is a catalytic force. All the various beings who travel between dimensions do so with either technological devices or magical powers. This is true of those in our Order, the Reality Patrol, the various criminal interdimensional travelers—"

"And the gods."

"And supernatural entities of numerous types, yes. Technology or magic, in every case. You do so without conscious spellcasting or intermetaphysical devices; therefore you create these gates with an innate power."

"I'm not saying I don't have some kind of knack," said Aleck. "I'm just saying I don't *create* the gates, I find them. I have Weird Luck, you know that."

"It's an epistemological question." Clark poked his finger toward the ground as though staking his assertion through the Idiranian carpet and into the stone floor. "In an infinite multiverse, is there even a difference between finding a world and creating it? There is no way to know for certain, and we are agreed that nobody quite knows the means by which you activate the gates—I will compromise by using the word 'activate.' But consider how many times you have passed through a gate that was entirely unknown before you found it...."

"Proves nothing."

"It *implies* plenty," said Clark. "You have an extraordinary power. But now you're demonstrating the same sort of thinking toward your powers that you use with your writing and art. The sort of thinking that keeps you from submitting your own work to the Archive. Your low self-opinion holds you back, and you mask your lack of results with arrogance. It's an outrage, Woad, I'll tell you that to your face."

"I know what you frickin' think. You bring it up every goddamn time I see you."

"It's ridiculous, especially for a man of your age. You have a compulsion, Woad."

"I'm a good ten years younger than I look."

Clark laughed, humorlessly. "It's embarrassing that you should have so much raw material and yet have nothing you are willing to publish in our Archive." Clark jabbed his finger toward Aleck's desk, in the corner, piled high with sketchbooks, notebooks, tapes, and discs, with an acoustic guitar lying precariously atop it all.

*Gesticulating like a little dictator,* Aleck thought again, looking at the guitar. *Hey, I can use that as a lyric!* "Ge-sti-cu-laaa-ting," he sang under his breath.

"What?" asked Clark.

"*Likealittle* dic-*taaaaa*-tor," he whispered. "You sound like Beth," Aleck said aloud. "Telling me how much I should have accomplished by such-and-such age."

"It's not your numerical age, Woad, it's your conviction. You have the conviction of an adolescent."

"Great, thanks." Aleck pouted. "Whatever."

"Here's a fun game for a youngster like you. Guess how old I am."

"What do you mean?"

"Guess my age."

"It's impossible to know, you ass. You've traveled on so many time streams, the question doesn't even make sense."

"I mean biologically, not chronologically." Clark smiled. "How old would you say I was, if you saw me in, say, your hometown, in Twentieth Century America? Where did you originate, again? A-5 New Mexico?"

"New Jersey."

"Twentieth Century New Jersey, Earth-A00005. Assume an adequate diet, full medical care given the available technology; how old am I?"

"I have no idea. Sixty? But who cares? Not even you have a clue." *Dic-taaaaa-tor*, he thought.

"Wrong," said Clark. "I have a Subjective Chronometer."

"What?"

"I know my age, as measured by my material form's experience of the passage of time. I can tell you my exact age right now."

"How can you do that? Some kind of meditation trick?"

Clark grinned. "A device. I obtained it on my first journey offworld, as a young man, when I departed Twenty-First Century Earth-X00023. I know what my age was when I left, of course. Adding the time that has passed subjectively for me since then, I am," he lowered his voice, "one hundred and seventeen years old."

Aleck laughed. "No way."

"Yes," said Clark. "Yes way."

"One hundred seven*teen*?" Aleck tugged at his beard. "How? Tech, not magic, I bet. Right? From Vasg, maybe. Or an Earth like A00005, Twenty-First Century or later."

"I have had the benefit of advanced medical techniques, yes," said Clark.

"I'm surprised I never knew that about you. No wonder you had time to write all those books."

"I wrote because I had conviction! I finished my works because I had a sense of dedication to our Order. It's an embarrassment that a man in your position should be unable to show his work, even his work-in-progress, to his peers."

"Give me a break."

"Your role carries responsibility, to set an example for the Order of Eight Directions! You are supposed to lead us, from here in the Archive, yet you don't have a single work of art or scholarship stored in it. While cretins like Chester fill it with garbage."

"The Archive has always contained erotica," countered Aleck.

Clark made a sour face. "You have contributed nothing to the Order but your sloth. Nothing but the personal letters you have written to those in the Order, and the rare reports about your activities, which have been properly filed in the Acting Archivists' Correspondence Room—over your protests, I might add!"

"Damn right!" Aleck flung his hand toward his desk. "When I die, you can root through that pile and do whatever you want with it. In the meantime, it's mine to do with as I please. You can have a book, or a drawing, or a song when I say it's finished, and not until then, you frickin' pushy and/ or grasping jerk."

"I have a theory." Clark clasped his hands and closing his eyes in mock reverie. "I believe that something specific is holding you back, Woad. Something has you trapped with the heart of a teenage boy. Something you experienced, dare I say it, when you *were* a teenage boy."

"Do tell." Aleck shook his head. "I'm sure I haven't heard this one about a hundred and seventeen fuckin' times from you before."

"Woad, really." Clark gave him a piercing stare. "Think about it. On your very first journey offworld, you unwittingly helped cause the massacre of hundreds in the city of Melkhaios. Ever since then, you've wanted to get back to Kaios-X00023 to make amends. That's why you became an interdimensional traveler to begin with."

"So if I have the ability to create gates at will, why haven't I ever been back?"

"I never said 'at will.'" Clark pointed his finger straight up, raising his bushy eyebrows.

"I didn't know you were a psychotherapist." Aleck realized he was jabbing his finger at Clark and forcefully pocketed both hands. "Okay. I admit that I'm kind of a pacifist because I saw some awful shit when I was a kid. I feel guilty sometimes about the Battle of Melkhaios. I carry that memory with me, I even still have nightmares once in a blue moon. But it's a total goddamn leap to say that's why I'm a perfectionist with my writing and music and stuff. I just want my submissions to be good, man!"

"I never said 'perfectionist,' Woad. Melkhaios is a void in your soul. Your failure there has branded you as a failure in your own heart. That is why you never finish anything: you never dare risk the shame of another failure." Clark lowered his voice. "But your method, never finishing anything, simply substitutes a *definitive* failure in place of the fearful uncertainty."

"Give it a rest." Aleck gritted his teeth.

*"I can help cure you of your past,"* whispered Clark.

"What?"

"My longevity, and my Subjective Chronometer device, come from a source that occasionally gives me access to other interesting technologies as well. I've stumbled upon one that I think will fascinate you." Clark held up the gate device he obtained from Chester and waggled it in the air.

"What is that?" asked Aleck. "That looks like a Reality Patrol gate gizmo. Where in hell did you get that?" He held out his hand.

"My connections." Clark smiled.

Aleck laughed. "You, Clark? I can't believe it! You're like a Boy Scout when it comes to Reality Patrol regulations. I never imagined you'd traffic in stolen Patrol gear!" He smiled at Clark.

Clark grinned back.

"Where did you get that thing? That looks like a high-end one, too—it's tiny. Most of their field agents have to make do with clunky steampunk junk compared to that baby. Let me see that thing, man." He reached for it. Clark pulled it back.

"Impetuous Woad, you're missing the best part. It's not the device. It's what's *in* it."

"What are you talking about." Aleck continued holding out his hand.

"Melkhaios," Clark said slowly.

"What about Meh—" said Aleck, realizing as he spoke exactly what Clark meant. Another pang of adrenaline shot into his hands and feet.

"I haven't tested it, mind you, but my sources claim this has been programmed with one set of coordinates: the city of Melkhaios, on the world of Kaios-X00023."

"When," said Aleck, his voice a dry whisper.

"The device will simply bypass the target world's Astral Web, of course."

Aleck cleared his throat. "When."

"Hmm?" asked Clark.

"When," said Aleck. "When?"

"You mean, at what point in history does this gate open?" Clark smiled.

"Yes!"

"Some time *before* the Battle of Melkhaios."

Aleck found himself trembling. "How long before?"

Clark shrugged and looked around the room. "Not long. They couldn't guarantee a particular time." He smiled and extended the device to Woad. "Perhaps a year?"

Aleck shook as though stuck outside in desperate cold weather. A year. Long enough to choreograph a far different future than the Battle of Melkhaios he had witnessed as a boy. A future without hundreds of civilians massacred by cannibals. And without that other thing, the thing he had never mentioned to Clark, nor his most trusted comrades in the Order, not even his dear wife Beth: his own death at the hands of the Reality Patrol. His one and only secret from her, but a doozy.

"Let's try it." Clark slipped the three small discs out of the large one and walked over to the doorway.

# The Acting Archivist's Wife

The door swung open, smacking Clark in the hand. He yelped. The discs clattered across the floor and slid under the shelves in a corner of the room. Aleck stood there watching, paralyzed with uncertainty.

Beth Woad stood in the doorway holding a bayonet. Salt-and-pepper dreadlocks, combat boots, black Ludicra t-shirt. "Oh, shit! Sorry, Clark!"

"No matter." He backed away from the bayonet, squeezing his hand and wincing.

"What brings you here?" she asked.

"Just paying a visit to our esteemed leader," said Clark.

"Let me help you get your stuff." Beth strode after the lost discs. Kneeling, she felt around under the corner shelves. The bayonet hung from her hand. Over her shoulder she spoke to her husband. "Aleck, I have the coolest news for you. I can't wait to tell you." She handed up the large disc to Clark.

"Thank you," he said, blowing dust off of it and sliding it into his jacket pocket.

"You can help, too, dick." She pointed at him with the bayonet.

"Oh!" Clark braced himself on a heavy wooden shelf and lowered himself to his knees.

"Guess what this is!" Beth stage-whispered to Aleck, shaking the bayonet.

"Big knife," said Aleck, coming out of his daze, grateful for some distraction from Clark's unthinkable claim about the gate. "Rifle bayonet?" Beth handed it to him, handle-first. He examined it, glad to focus on it rather than his one secret from his wife. "This is for one of them Earth projectile rifles, see, the barrel goes through here." He stuck the tip of his finger through the hole in the crossguard.

Clark swept under a shelf with his hand and drew forth a wad of dust the size of a rat. "Oh!" He began sneezing.

"You gotta be careful under there. My man's not known for his dusting."

"See how it clips onto the rifle?" continued Aleck, working the catch over and over. "This is like First-Half Twentieth Century, World War One or Two. I love this tech. Check out this mechanism." He pointed the pommel at Beth, working the heavy catch with his thumb. *Clunk*. "Isn't that sweet design?"

He didn't meet her eyes. He had to tell her about his possible impending death. And ask forgiveness for hiding it.

*Not in front of Clark.*

*So just tell him to fuck off....*

"So simple," said Beth, nodding. "So solid."

"Just one little moving part and a heavy spring inside," said Aleck. "That knife is never going to come off your rifle if you don't want it to, and that catch is never going to break. Man, the tools folks made when they had motives other than mere profit."

"So would Jack Waghalter's rifle use something like that?"

"Waghalter." Clark wiped his nose with a handkerchief. "The famed 'Cannibal-King' on whom your husband is so fixated. We were just speaking of the revolution on Melkhaios."

"Never mind that!" Aleck glared at him. "No, this is for a heavy bolt-action or semi-automatic war gun. Waghalter's rifle Victoria is a little lever-action hunting carbine. This is probably the same kind of bayonet he had, though."

"I thought you said it didn't fit his rifle," said Beth.

"No no he had his grandfather's bayonet," said Aleck. "From the Spanish Civil War. Just before World War Two. Part of World War Two, really. But that bayonet didn't fit Victoria, he just used it by hand."

"I'm fuckin' with you." Beth laughed. "That *is* Jack Waghalter's bayonet."

Aleck stared at her.

"Really." She looked at him earnestly. "Doomer just dropped it off. He brought it back from Eighty-Seventh Century Earth."

"No way."

"Yes. Doomer got it from Waghalter's heir in the year 8661 on Earth-X00023."

"Impossible." Aleck worked the catch-release mechanism some more. "This is too well preserved. It could be sixty years old, but not six thousand."

"You just said it would never break," said Beth.

"Dude," said Aleck. "This knife is not six thousand years old."

Beth laughed again. "I'm fuckin' with you. Waghalter kept it in an extradimensional pocket. It *is* about sixty years old, from its own perspective. Waghalter stored it outside space-time, except for the occasional moments when he was using it. And it stayed outside space-time after he died, till his Eighty-Seventh Century heir retrieved it."

"Why the hell would his heir give it to Doomer?" asked Aleck, still incredulous. With both hands he placed the bayonet carefully atop the Wall of Athan.

"Jack's umpteen-great grandson, or whoever he was, said the thing was cursed." Beth shrugged. "Doomer convinced the guy the Order could remove the curse."

"One might say that your obsession with Melkhaios is as much an obsession with Waghalter," said Clark.

"Give it a rest!" said Aleck.

"What's the gizmo?" Beth handed Clark two of the small discs. "Looks like top-shelf Reality Patrol issue." She looked at Aleck.

Aleck sighed deeply. No sense trying to hide the gate's supposed destination; truly, he needed her partnership. They needed to think this through together. He pointed at the discs in Clark's hand. "Motherfucker expects us to believe it's a gate to Pre-Revolutionary Melkhaios."

Beth frowned at him. "You believe him."

"What if, though? We could stop the massacres...." *Oh yeah, and maybe I'll die.*

Beth looked at Clark, who smiled. "Where the hell did you get it? Patrol give it to you? As a trap for us?"

"Chester gave it to me, actually," said Clark, unfazed. "He thought your husband might be interested in it, and asked me to pass it on to you."

"And Chester got it from whom?"

Clark shrugged.

Beth scowled at Aleck. "So you wanna try to change Melkhaios history, and you think you're going to actually redirect it into something you'll feel happy about."

"What else can we do but try?" Aleck felt numb with guilt at the secret of his possible death. *Just tell her, jerkoff.*

"You're telling me you want us to go through an untested gate, which by the way looks very much like a frickin' Reality Patrol gate, that you just get from this *dude*," pointing at Clark, "who totally wants you out of the way so he can take your job?"

"Beth," said Aleck. "Whatever. Let's check out the gate first, the whole thing's moot unless it's real anyway."

"Your whole reason for going there is to change things. What if you change *our* past?"

Aleck looked at her. "Yeah, but consider what's at stake for the people of Melkhaios..."

Clark cleared his throat. They turned to see him standing beside the door. "I managed to find the final disc, while you youngsters were having your debate." He gestured to the glittering discs attached at the four corners of the door. "I have arranged our test. Shall we see if it works?"

He opened the door.

# Another Archive

Beyond the doorway, a hallway stretched to right and left, almost exactly like the one outside Aleck's smoking room: the same vaulted stone of light gray, with no visible mortar or even seams between stones. However, instead of Aleck's posters of Pink Floyd, Deep Purple, and Black Sabbath decorating the wall across from the door, there stood a tall stone statue of a man in a robe.

Aleck stared.

"Whoa," said Beth. "Is that really the original Archive in Melkhaios?"

"I know that face." Aleck pointed at the statue. "That's Kaios the Summoner."

"Really?" Clark swept through the doorway. He looked up and down the hallway, and, seeing no one, walked up to the statue. "You met him when you were in this world as a youth?" He stood with arms crossed, admiring the statue.

"No, he was long dead. I saw his face carved on the mountain."

"Long dead?" Clark continued looking at the statue. "Ah, yes—he died when the Archive went interdimensional."

"Vice-versa." Aleck turned to Beth. "Hold that door, would you?" He hurriedly crossed the room back to his desk.

"We going somewhere?" she asked.

Aleck grabbed a small shoulder-slung courier bag and began filling it with gear: notebook and pen, personal stereo and headphones, miniature video camera, a tiny solid-state Dictaphone device.... He looked about the room for other useful items.

"Aleck."

He looked at her and took a deep breath. "Beth...."

"Baby, you're doing that tunnel vision thing, like bigtime."

"Look." Aleck took another deep breath.

"I've always speculated that you have a mild case of autism," called Clark from the hall, still examining the statue of Kaios.

Aleck frowned at him. "Autism's not a disease, jackass, and who knows if that's my deal, or any of a number of other equally healthy neurological variations." He looked back at Beth. "You know me. You know how much time I've spent thinking about this." He gestured around his den. "All this stuff—everything in this room.... I've collected all this bullshit just as a side effect of trying to get back to this place."

"Obsessive-Compulsive, then," said Clark over his shoulder, with a little laugh.

Aleck ignored him. "The whole reason we're here, the whole reason I ever became Acting Archivist, is because I've been trying to get back to Melkhaios. I have to do this."

"Do *what*, exactly?" asked Beth.

"Prevent all them people getting killed!" Aleck waved his hands in the air. "Best I ever dared hoped for was to make up for it after the fact in some limited way. But if we land before the revolution even starts, we can actually stop the massacres from happening!" He broke his gaze from Beth and began stalking around the room, putting knickknacks into his shoulder bag.

"Yeah, you're not listening. How?"

"The Reality Patrol won't be pleased." Clark stood in the doorway with his hands folded. "Mrs. Woad is right."

Beth glowered at him.

"The gate's *in* the Archive." Aleck took a small polished stone from a shelf, dusted it on the thigh of his ripped jeans, and put it in his pocket. He resumed searching. "They can't find the Archive. Nobody can, if their intent is hostile to the Archive's purpose. It's an ontological fact." He dropped a stolen Reality Patrol force-grenade into his shoulder bag.

"Is that your antimagic grenade?" asked Beth.

"Just a force-grenade. Just in case."

"The Patrol can detect you tampering with the fate of a foreign world," said Clark. "The Archive protects you little when you are *outside* of it."

"Whose side are you on?" Aleck stood up from a wooden box full of small plastic toys and gave Clark a helpless look. "They can only detect anything if they're actively scanning that world!"

"Aleck! What makes you think they're not doing just that?" Beth crossed the room and stared him in the eye. "You aren't fucking thinking. You don't have any idea where that thing came from. *Clark hates you.*"

"Madam, please," said Clark.

"You want his gig." Beth turned back to Aleck. "He thinks you're incompetent and irresponsible, and he'd hand you over to the Reality Patrol in a second if he knew he could do it without getting burned by them in the process. And you don't even know where that gate actually leads to! That could be a Reality Patrol jail cell with Melkhaios décor!"

"Give me a break!" Aleck turned away from her and resumed scanning his shelves.

"And even if it is Melkhaios, what the hell are we going to do? Parlay a fucking truce?"

"You *know* we always have to improvise!" said Aleck. "We'll see what tactics make sense once we get a chance to assess the conditions!" He looked up at a stuffed crow on a shelf above his desk, and spoke the word "*Thoth!*" at it. It stretched its wings, cawed once, and flew over to Aleck's shoulder. He pointed. "Scan the background radiation coming from the world beyond that gate, and compare it to what your data banks have on Kaios-X00023."

"Understood," croaked the crow, and flew out the door. It landed on the head of the statue and cocked its head this way and that.

"Look," said Beth. "We've always agreed to 'use our powers for good,' but you know shit doesn't scale. It's no different from mundane power. We do small-scale actions and projects where we can actually guide the results a little, not big paternalistic world-changing shit of the sort that goes sideways, right out the gate, every damn time. 'Stay close to the ground,' like it says in the Order's Manifesto. Plus this whole white savior thing is empire-building bullshit in its own right. You know this."

"But the whole point is this already happened!" said Aleck. "I saw it!"

"Yeah, exactly. You saw the standard white savior haywire bloodbath."

"And exactly, the point is to change it!"

"With a *slightly* different mass-murdering superhero from a slightly different American Empire? Marvelous plan."

"Jesus, Beth, we've talked a million times about how simply picking the best possible Waghalter to play Cannibal-King counts as 'staying close to the ground.'"

"*You've* talked about it a million times, while I listen and say 'maybe.' The simplest version of this plan still involves juggling ninety-nine things at once."

"Sure, there are a lot of pieces to it, but we know this backwards and forwards!"

"Let's pick one," said Beth. "The Skull of Kaios. You say the Skull of Kaios was broken, and that might've resulted in bringing a psycho Waghalter that gave free rein to all the havoc. So you aim to walk through that door and prevent it from getting broken. Right?"

"Exactly!" An idea came to Aleck, and he snapped his fingers. He rolled his desk chair over to a bookcase and stood up on it. The chair slid and rocked slightly underfoot as he took down a small chest of carved wood from the top shelf. He sat down in the chair with the chest in his lap, and opened it.

"Okay, how?"

Aleck drew something made from gray cloth out of the chest. "Huh?"

"How," repeated Beth. "How are you going to prevent the Skull from breaking?"

"You know, go find Akaz, and get *him* to make sure it doesn't happen. This is a gate to the *past*, Beth. I saw us do this. You and I show up, we team up with Akaz, we summon the Cannibal-King, and that catalyzes the revolution. We just have to be more careful about who we summon."

"For all we know, trying to summon the Cannibal-King is what breaks the Skull! Or even just walking through that door! And do we really know for sure that the broken Skull even has anything to do with what went wrong? It's an interesting guess, but seriously, it's wildly speculative, baby."

"The broken Skull has to at least be part of it. How could it not?" Aleck put the gray cloth into his bag and stood up, leaving the carved wooden chest on the office chair.

"Aleck, my point is that it makes no sense to just barge through there." Beth turned to Clark. "Where did Chester get this gate."

"He wouldn't say," said Clark. "You know Chester: many words, little content. But I gather, from little hints among his evasions, that he *stole* it from a Reality Patrolman."

"You mean it's *hot*?"

Clark frowned and shrank slightly. "That is exactly why Chester asked me to bring it here: because the Patrol can never find the Archive."

"You don't know that!"

"Sure we do," said Aleck, "come on."

Clark frowned deeper. "It is an ontological fact, young lady. Fully documented in both theory and history."

"It's not an 'ontological fact,' you pompous goose," said Beth. "And history and theory don't dictate the limits of what's possible! You guys amaze me. Aleck, I've wandered through countless undocumented interdimensional gates with you, we did hella reckless shit in our twenties. But this takes the absolute cake."

"Look," said Aleck, "the gate's open *now*. We have no idea how long it'll be open, or whether we'll be able to open it again."

"Exactly my point! I wasn't planning on getting stuck forever on an unknown world today!"

Aleck heaved a sigh. "Clark, how long will that gizmo run?"

Clark raised an eyebrow. "It presumably can't last for long, considering its size. But the Reality Patrol have reliable equipment; that much can be said for them." He stepped to the side of the doorway and gestured through it. "I would suggest, however, not to leave it open for too long."

"This is a setup," said Beth through clenched teeth.

"Thoth," Aleck said to the crow, "what do you have for me?"

"Definitely an X-world," said the crow in its croaky voice. "The Astral Plane bears the radiation signature from the Cycle of Cataclysm."

"And that's a statue of Kaios the Summoner you're standing on."

"Kaios the Summoner," said the crow, "also known as Kaios Spirit-Tamer, Kaios the Master-Builder, etc. Mortal manifestation of the Sun Dragon; founder of the City of Melkhaios; founder of the Archive; whose death catalyzed the First Cataclysm, also known as the Great Breach, i.e., the first local manifestation of the Cycle of Cataclysm."

Aleck looked at Beth. "It's Kaios-X00023."

Beth walked up to Aleck, took his hands in her hands, looked into his eyes. "Baby, it's a setup." She looked at Clark. "Just look at him. Like a spider, waiting."

"Mrs. Woad, I resent your attitude toward me."

Beth made a small shooing gesture at him and looked back at Aleck. "What are you going to do, enlist Akaz in your plan?"

"Of course. I saw us all together back when I was a kid! We *know* we go through here anyway! We just have to do a better job of convincing him to take the consequences into account."

"You told me you saw your future self arguing with Akaz about the massacres." Beth squeezed his hands. "What in the name of god makes you think you're going to be able to make anything different happen? The evidence says otherwise, plain as day. If you want to make a real difference, just *don't go*."

"Yeah, but Beth. Remember, when I was a teenager, my future self said events were occurring slightly differently than he remembered."

"But you also said he was trying his damnedest to change things, and he failed. This is an X-world, with a high likelihood of Meta-Novikov self-consistency across parallels—especially when it comes to cataclysmic events. You can't just flick it aside with a deftly executed butterfly effect. The future cataclysm will still tend to draw all threads of fate into itself."

"C'mon, let's at least take a look." Aleck turned and walked out through the doorway.

"Aleck!" said Beth, chasing after him.

Clark shut the door behind them and tapped the gate's off switch.

# Bone Council

Aleck and Beth stopped in their tracks. They looked at each other, then back at the closed door. Beth shoved the door open. Through the doorway they saw not Aleck's smoking room, but a large, circular, sunlit room with a dozen carved obelisks standing in a circle. Tall windows showed a choppy bay of dark water, a city of white stone, and a gray mountain with a titanic stone face carved into it. In the opposite direction, far across the bay, stood a distant castle of tall towers, seemingly built on top of a massive bridge spanning the mouth of the bay.

Aleck's heart raced. *So this is it, then? Surprise, guess what, it's time to fix Melkhaios?*

"Shit," said Beth.

"Let me try it." Aleck pulled the door shut and then re-opened it. They saw the same room with the obelisks. "Dammit," he said.

"Tell me you've got a key to the Archive on you."

"I think I have at least one of them." Aleck hurriedly rummaged in his shoulder bag. "I wanted to come here, not get fucking *stranded* here, Clark. That son of a bitch."

"I told you so," said Beth. "I'm going to kill him when I get my hands on him."

"He's right," said Aleck. He pulled out the wadded-up gray cloth and tucked it under his arm, to more easily look through the rest of the stuff in his bag. "Clark's right. He would make a better Acting Archivist than me."

"Clark wouldn't get tricked into going through a gate, I'll grant him that." Beth grabbed the cloth from under Aleck's arm and shook it out to reveal the outlines of a robe made from a strange, lightweight fabric. "Keeper Robe?"

Aleck checked his pants pockets and pulled out the Chrome Five. "Sweet! Here's the First Key. That stupid son of a bitch didn't count on this." He shut the door, held the Five tightly in his left hand, and opened the door again.

They looked into the room of obelisks.

"Uh."

Aleck closed the door, slapped the Five against its surface, and held it there while reopening it. Obelisks.

Faint voices and footsteps echoed down the hall, approaching. "Shit!" Beth pulled Aleck into the room and pushed the door shut. "Shit a lot!"

"Beth." Aleck stared at the door. "Why didn't my key work?"

"Come on." She tugged at his elbow. "If they're coming in here, whoever they are, we need to get hid quick."

They crossed the room. The obelisks stood at different heights and in varying states of repair, some of them just fragments held together with metal rods like restored sculptures in a museum. Each pillar had a single line of text carved into it, winding around and around in a tight spiral. Aleck had heard of these from Akaz: the Books of

Kaios. At least one of them contained parts of the prophecy of the Cannibal-King. Beth pulled Aleck behind a mostly-intact obelisk far from the door, and threw the Keeper Robe over them both.

"Shit!" said Aleck. "We left the Crow Terminal out in the hall."

Beth shushed him just as the door opened. Their eyes met. *Here we are again*, thought Aleck, certain Beth was thinking more or less the same thing, *hiding side by side for the hundredth time.*

They heard someone enter the room.

"It doesn't really smell like a crow," said a deep, resonant voice that struck Aleck as naggingly familiar.

"Well, whatever it is," came the soft voice of a very old man or woman, "it seems auspicious to coincide with your visit."

Several soft thumps echoed from the middle of the room, like large pillows thrown to the floor.

"We'll see, Elder," said the deep voice. "The crow feathers are real enough. But it's not crow on the inside. It smells very strange. It reminds me of something from my vision."

"Clearly, then, an auspicious sign," said the Elder, "to appear outside our council door, just when you arrive from afar to tell us of your visions."

"It's not that far," said the deep voice.

Aleck peeked around the side of the pillar, keeping the hem of the Robe over his head. In the middle of the room, two figures stood beside a pile of large pillows on the floor: someone in a gray robe, with huge eyes and blue-green skin, and the Cook from Corpsewater, holding the Crow Terminal. The Cook stood seven feet tall, his beech-gray skin covered with whorls and jags of slate-gray tattooing, his leaf-green braids tied atop his head in a haphazard crest. He wore only rawhide pants; tucked into his rawhide belt was a golden bone wrapped in strings of beads, which Aleck recognized as one of the Shinbones of Kaios. He was about to step forth with a "Hey, Cook!" when he remembered that the Cook had not met him yet—Aleck's arrival as a teenager would happen sometime in the future. More people in gray robes entered the room, carrying pillows. Aleck ducked his head back.

Aleck and Beth huddled under the robe behind the pillar, listening. People exchanged greetings and bantered. Now and then Aleck heard the gently croaking voice of the Elder asking, "Are we all here yet?" or "Who's still missing?" Beth peeked around the side of the pillar, keeping the hem of the Robe carefully over her head, and retreated. Her eyes met Aleck's. She shrugged. Aleck peered around his side of the pillar and saw a dozen gray-robed Keepers and the Cook arranging pillows and seating themselves in a circle. He ducked back.

"Before we begin," rumbled the deep voice of the Cook, "I'd like to ask about this. I found it perched on top of the statue of Kaios in the hall."

"Looks like a crow," someone said.

"Yes, but it isn't," said the Cook.

"Dead crow?" suggested someone. Several people laughed.

"A dead crow is still a crow," said someone else.

"It's not a crow on the inside," said the Cook. "It smells like sawdust and metal. And something burnt I don't recognize. It's got no trace of the bay on it, so it didn't fly here from shore. Not recently, anyway."

"Really?" asked the Elder. "It couldn't be one of the Archivist's Crow Terminals, could it? Those haven't been seen since the Great Breach!"

The Cook sniffed at the Crow Terminal.

"Why is it called a 'Crow Terminal'?" asked someone.

"What's a 'terminal'?" asked another.

"That's the name given in the old records," said the Elder. "I remember researching the matter once, long ago, but I never found an adequate explanation of the term. Only a description of their purpose."

"It smells like old Archive dust," said the Cook. "I'd say it's been here a long, long time. It smells faintly of a person, too, but no one I recognize."

Others in the room continued asking questions of the Cook. "What sort of person?"

The Cook sniffed again. "A Normal, maybe. Nobody wild or amphibious. Wait." He sniffed. "Diggly-Weed!" He laughed. "My head is saturated with so much Diggly-Weed-smoke, I didn't even notice it."

"So it belongs to a Diggly, then?"

"A weed-smoker," said the Cook. "Not necessarily a Diggly."

"Could this have anything to do with what you came to tell us, Cook?" asked someone.

"Don't know. The Elder Keeper thought it auspicious for a crow to appear just now, me being a Wilder, but I have no idea."

"What is the Crow Terminal supposed to do, aside from look like a crow and smell like smoke and sawdust?"

Laughter.

"Nothing to do with the Corvus Drive?" This elicited gasps from more than one Keeper, and nearly from Aleck and Beth as well: they knew of a technomagical artifact with that name, a horrifically dangerous one.

"Nothing of the sort," said the Elder. "The Archivist could simply see and speak through his Crow Terminals."

"Try it," said someone.

"Try what?" asked someone else.

"Yes, see if you can speak to the Archivist through it!" said a third.

"Archivist!" said the Elder in a resonant, croaky voice. "Great Thoth, eternal Keeper of our Archive! Can you hear me?"

A long moment of silence followed.

"I say we forget about it for now."

"Let's get on with the Bone Council."

"What if someone's using it to spy on us?"

"Using it how? It doesn't do anything."

"Let us begin," said the Elder. "Cook, please be so kind as to place it in the middle with the Sacred Bone. Are there any objections?"

Several people said No, while others muttered or whispered briefly; then silence. A sound broke the silence that Aleck knew must be the clatter of beads as the Cook rattled the Shinbone of Kaios. Then a long silence followed.

Aleck peered around the side of the pillar. The Cook and the dozen Keepers sat there, the Crow Terminal and Shinbone of Kaios resting in the middle of the circle. No one moved. Aleck ducked back. Beth looked at him. He shrugged. Beth looked around the other side of the pillar for a moment, then turned back to Aleck, her brow furrowed in bafflement. He shrugged again.

The silence continued.

Beth and Aleck simultaneously looked around the sides of the pillar, Beth tugging the corner of the Robe from Aleck's grip. He jerked back behind the column. While re-draping the robe over him, Beth mouthed the word "Sorry!" Aleck soundlessly puffed out of his cheeks and raised his eyebrows.

The silence of the Bone Council continued.

Aleck's eyes strayed over the lines of text carved into the surface of the pillar. *English!* Akaz had told him there was a reason why the people of Kaios-X00023 spoke English, but never explained what it was. Seeing the writing on the pillar startled him. As a boy he had spoken English with folk of all sorts on Kaios-X00023, seen it on a few signs and buildings in Melkhaios, but he never saw a book or a block of text when he was here before. It seemed incongruous and eerie. *Why in god's name do they speak English?* he thought. He looked at Beth, who was reading the patch of pillar in front of her. *Damn it, Beth, I need to talk to you.... I wish we had those telepaphones from Eighty-Seventh Century Earth, why didn't I grab those? Dammit, why didn't you help me pack before we went through that door...?* He scowled, unable to kid himself that the blame laid itself anywhere but at the feet of his needless, manic hurry. She had done everything to rein him in short of throwing him to the ground and pinning him. He turned to face the pillar. *I wish these clowns would start whatever it is they're doing.*

He read:

*...Beware the third of them: shaking a bone-rattle, he stabs you with arrows. He rallies the secret teachers to harbor your undoing....*

Beads clattered against the metal Shinbone of Kaios, shocking Aleck. He jumped and started to exclaim, a "Wh—" (of "What the—!") exploding from his mouth before he could stifle it. Beth looked at him, wide-eyed. They froze. The rattle continued—it had covered the sound of Aleck's voice. They both exhaled silently with relief.

Aleck jabbed his finger at the word "bone-rattle" and mouthed the words, "I just read this!"

"What?" mouthed Beth.

"This! It's about the Cook!"

"What?" Beth, irritated, craned her neck to read what Aleck was pointing at, raised her eyebrows, furrowed them and looked at Aleck. She pointed toward the sound of the shinbone rattle. Aleck nodded, vigorously. Beth raised her eyebrows again.

The rattle stopped. "Friends," said the Cook. "It is my honor and pleasure to conduct this Council. In the manner of your custom, please feel free to say 'Hoy, hoy,' to induce assent with the spirit of the speaker. I request the freedom to express emphatic assent, as is my people's custom, with the word 'Boum.'"

"Hoy, hoy," said several of the Keepers. "Boum," said one. Laughter.

"I have requested this Council in order to reveal to you the visions I have lately beheld in rattle-trance. Fragments have pieced themselves together. Now I must seek not only your wisdom and skill, but also your alliance."

The Cook paused for a moment. Aleck heard faint rattling sounds, as though he were slowly turning the Shinbone over and over in his hands, thinking how to continue.

"As carved into these pillars of prophecy, Kaios the Summoner foretold the Cannibal-King and his First Herald, who are not of our world, but who manifest to us from an overworld known simply as 'Earth.' Kaios told us of the Master Summoner, also from this Earth, who calls our King to us. He told us about the wonders of Earth, with its 'cars' and 'guns'; and the Cannibal-King, he said, will come to us with cars and guns to free us from these last remaining dregs of the Empire."

"Hoy, hoy," sounded several voices in approval.

"Friends," the Cook said, "I believe I have seen visions of both the First Herald and the Master Summoner. I believe I have unraveled a mystery about them, which the scholars of the prophecies have debated for four hundred years."

Quiet in the room.

"And I feel certain that these figures are coming soon."

The room filled with silent tension.

"Kaios used the same phrase—'A sunburst of scars etched on half his face'—in describing both the First Herald, a teenage boy, and the Master Summoner, a gray-haired old man."

A chill ran through Aleck's body. Beth squeezed his hand.

"Allow me to describe to you what I have seen." The Cook began tapping the rattle on the floor, very gently, in a steady rhythm. "I saw an Earth-boy traveling in a mule-less wagon, a 'car,' and I saw this car hit a tree so hard that both tree and car were broken. And the car stopped so suddenly that the boy flew out through the front of it. I saw this boy, bleeding from his face, walk through Bitchwood and dive into the healing-pool at Corpsewater. And when he emerged from the caresses of the Corpsewater Nymph, he had a sunburst of scars etched across half of his face. This was the First Herald."

The Cook remained silent for a little while, continuing to tap the rattle.

"Also I saw a man with gray hair. I saw him here, in your Archive. He spoke to me and he said, in plain language, 'I have come to summon the Cannibal-King.'"

"Hoy, hoy," came several voices.

"He had the same sunburst of scars. He was older, but his pattern of scars the exact same. And he said more: he said, 'When I was here as a boy, I witnessed the summoning of the wrong Cannibal-King. I have come back into the past to set things right.'"

Bodies rustled uncomfortably.

"You hear me truly. The First Herald and the Master Summoner are one and the same. So saith the Shinbone of Kaios." He rattled the Shinbone loudly and then returned to the gentle tapping rhythm.

No one spoke for a long while. Aleck's mind reeled with what he was hearing. *What are the odds of us landing here and now?* he asked himself, as he routinely did under outlandishly improbable circumstances. Then as always, he answered: *Goddamn Weird Luck.* He frowned at Beth.

*Sure wish we could have a little chat right about now.* She mouthed some words he couldn't make out, and seemed to be gesturing for them to step out from behind the pillar. "Wait and see," he mouthed, shaking his head. "Make sure it's safe."

"What?"

Aleck shook his head emphatically.

"The implications are simple," said the Cook. "Several ambiguities of scripture are explained. More importantly, this means that we have been seeking the wrong person."

Bodies rustled uncomfortably in their robes.

"Your Order has always assumed that the First Herald was first to arrive. His arrival presages that of the Master Summoner, who then summons the Cannibal-King, who unites the armies of the wild folk. But no. The Master Summoner has come back in time to change history. I know you understand this idea, of traveling in time, for it was here among you that I learned of it. If he has gone back in time to change history, then he will surely aim for a time before his arrival as the First Herald."

Bodies rustled uncomfortably. No one spoke. The Cook tapped the rattle rhythmically. Aleck felt as though he were missing something. Clearly the Cook was talking about him, but what was he saying, exactly? That the Keepers should be on the lookout for him. But to help him change history, or to hinder him?

Aleck's gaze drifted across a line of text on the pillar:

*...And it was I who tilted the Watcher's ships,' said the Master Summoner, 'though when I bring the Canni-*

*bal-King, he will do more than tilt. He will bring smiting fire. His weapon is named Victory....*

*This has gotta be the weirdest Weird Luck I've ever had,* Aleck said to himself. *I stumble into a room in another universe, and not only am I the topic of conversation, but there's carvings about me in ancient stone. Not to mention we were just talking about 'Victoria,' Waghalter's rifle....*

He couldn't read any further along that line without poking his head around the side of the pillar, so he skipped to the next line:

*...I have come to shape history,' said the Master Summoner....*

A chip in the stone beside the word "shape" seemed to efface part of the word. *Did it originally say something else?* Thought Aleck. "Reshape"? Could be. "Unshape"? *That doesn't sound great!* he thought. He kept reading:

*...to balance the scales, I will bring the Cannibal-King. The Tree of Life needs adjusting: the Watcher must be taken from Spheres and Keys unsuited to his true nature....*

He skipped to the next line:

*...no one but the Sun Dragon and Earth Dragon can dictate result. All our efforts, whatever our intent, whatever our insight, will land where the Dragons throw them.*

*We can but cast our deeds into the vortex....*

*Cast our deeds into the vortex?* thought Aleck. *That sounds bleak. Good god, what are we doing here? What the hell do I think I'm going to be able to accomplish? Summon a Cannibal-King who's somehow also some kinda Prince-o'- Peace?* Beth squeezed his hand again, pulling him out of his reverie. The Cook still tapped the rattle.

"Therefore, in order to best influence the outcome of the summoning, your Order should be expecting a gray-haired old man with sunburst scars, well before the arrival of the young man with sunburst scars. Otherwise, by the time you find the boy, the old man may already be lost to the clutches of the Watcher, Summoner and hence King alike lost to us." The tapping stopped. They heard the Cook put the Sacred Bone down, presumably in the middle of the circle.

"Why don't you go out there?" said Beth with the faintest breath.

"No way!" he said, just mouthing the words. "We need to see more!"

"What?"

"What if hooking up with these guys is what leads to the evil Cannibal-King? I have to hear more!"

"What?"

He shook his head.

There lasted a long silence. Eventually they heard someone pick up the rattle. Then another pause.

"To clarify," came the voice of a young man with a stuffed-up nose, "you are saying that the First Herald will come here from Earth as a boy, witness the summoning of an evil Cannibal-King, return to Earth, grow old, and return here—as the Master Summoner, arriving *before* his previous arrival. Correct?"

"Hoy, hoy," said the Cook.

"And the Master Summoner," said the stuffed-up boy, "then attempts to summon a different Cannibal-King, from a different Earth."

"Hoy, hoy."

"Then what happens to the original, evil Cannibal-King? And what happens to the Master Summoner who summoned him?"

He paused. They could hear him turning the Sacred Bone over and over in his hands. He put it down. Soon they heard it picked up again, and a woman asked, "How was the evil Cannibal-King ever summoned to begin with, unless it was by a Summoner who had seen him as a boy, and come back to summon a good King, and then failed?" She put down the Bone. Someone picked it up.

"Cook," said the Elder, "I will never dispute the accuracy of your visions. But I must agree with my colleagues. I am unclear of your analysis. Your admonition to stay vigilant for the arrival of the Master Summoner is duly noted. The co-identity of the Summoner and the First Herald is important to know, if it is so. However, the sequence of events you describe seems paradoxical. It loops back on itself infinitely. Who was the first Summoner? Had he not also been First Herald and witnessed an evil Cannibal-King? If not, then it would seem that the Summoner would have to have then contrived to summon himself as a boy, in order to witness the summoning of the evil King.... In truth, it hurts my head to think on it." He put down the Sacred Bone.

Silence swept across the room. No breathing or rustling of robes could be heard. Aleck's mind reeled. He now needed not only to summon the Cannibal-King, but also his young self? *What if worrying about summoning my younger self distracts me from the Cannibal-King project, causing me to summon the wrong one?* He ground his teeth. The silence continued. Aleck read some more text on the pillar:

*...said the Master Summoner to the First Herald. "I shall never rest, nor shall I cease, however many lives I must lead, however many thousands of times I must return to this same spot; never shall I abandon my effort until every soul of every living thing has been freed...."*

Aleck, absorbed in the text and its implications, had read his way around the pillar and out from under the Robe. He stood there, in plain view of the Cook and the dozen Keepers sitting in Bone Council.

# Interlude in Aleck's Smoking Room

Clark lay back against the doorway, shivering and sweating. His telepaphone rang.

*Hello.*

*We've registered his entry,* came the thoughts of Agent Xax. *And we're blocking his exit.*

*Well. Congratulations.*

*You feel guilty,* said Agent Xax. *I can sense it.*

*That is because I don't trust you, Xax. If you kill Woad or his wife, I'm complicit.*

*I think it's a good bit more than complicity.* Agent Xax laughed, then his tone turned serious. *I'm an investigator, Clark, not an assassin.*

*So you say. What you don't say is, 'Of course, Professor Clark, we wouldn't dream of letting them come to harm in any way.'*

*'Of course, Clark,'* said Agent Xax, *'we wouldn't dream of...'* what the—?

*'What the' what?*

Then Clark had a vision of a white cargo van flying across the night sky. Jagged forks of lightning erupted from it, blinding him. He fell against the door.

Static on the telepaphone.

He broke the connection and called the Archivist.

# The Master Summoner

No one said a word, but the faces of those gathered in the room reflected myriad emotions: awe, joy, bafflement. Aleck's heart stuttered in his chest and waves of chills swarmed through his body. Without taking his eyes off of Aleck, the Cook leaned over and picked up the Bone. "So ends this Bone Council." He shook the Bone. "Please thank the Bone."

"Thank you, Bone," said most of the Keepers with varying levels of enthusiasm, everyone still looking at Aleck.

"You are the Master Summoner." The Cook pointed the Sacred Bone at Aleck.

Aleck stifled the impulse to check on Beth and thereby give her away. If this were the situation he needed to avoid—if this meeting would lead to the summoning of an evil Cannibal-King—he'd need her help to escape. Fortunately she had the Keeper Robe. When Aleck had worn it among the Wilders, he learned that its magic affected all senses; it would hide her even from the Cook's superhuman sense of smell. *God,* he prayed silently, *if you fucking exist, thank you for Beth, my amazing wife who has saved my ass so many times, now please fucking protect her....* Surely she would stay hidden, keep her ears open, find them a way out if need be.

So, Aleck stalled. "Huh?" He found himself simply playing dumb. His panic made this not much of a stretch, with so much of his mind shut down by fear. "What?"

"I thought you would be older." The Cook stood up and tucked the Bone into his belt. "But your scars are those from my vision. And the hair." He walked closer. "And your eyes." The Cook stood uncomfortably close, towering over Aleck. "And your scent, most definitely. The scent of the First Herald from my rattle-trance." He bent slightly and sniffed near Aleck's scalp. "Yes, it is you I smelled on the Crow Terminal. And you also somehow smell like a Keeper." He straightened his posture and cocked his head at Aleck, looking at him with one eye. "Why do you smell like a Keeper? Are there Keepers on Earth?" He sniffed again.

"Keepers?"

"Understand, friend, you are the Master Summoner whether you know it or not. You have come to summon the Cannibal-King and free us from Apraxos."

"How the heck am I supposed to do that?"

The Elder replied. "With the Engines of Kaios, in the depths of our Archive."

"With the aid of Great Akaz," said the Cook.

"How do you know this Cannibal-King will do what you want?" asked Aleck, sharper than he intended, unable to resist sowing the seed of the idea but uncomfortably aware of breaking character from the innocent, ignorant goofus he'd been trying to portray.

Silence hung in the room. The Keepers looked at one another. The Cook looked at the Elder. The Elder nodded.

"That task is your fate," said the Cook, "not ours."

A chill crawled its way up Aleck's spine. "Mine?" He grasped for the solace of playing dumb again. "Uh, w-why me?"

"Indeed, this is the question asked by my vision," said the Cook. "Why would you want to summon him? The Prophecy of the Cannibal-King tells us only that it is your fate, and your deepest desire. Thus wrote Kaios. My vision tells of you coming here, traveling strangely in time, to right wrongs you witnessed as a boy before they come to pass. This much I assume you overheard, from behind the pillar." The Cook pointed.

"What?" *Don't mention my death dude don't mention my death dude don't mention my death.* Feeling quite unconvinced by himself, he added, weakly, "Huh?"

"Perhaps you are pretending not to understand." The Cook cocked his head again. "Do you test us? Or perhaps you fear we are dangerous to you? We are your allies completely in this."

"No idea what you're talking about, man." Aleck found his own delivery wooden and unconvincing.

"Is your wife afraid of us?" The Cook gestured at the pillar Beth was hiding behind.

"I'm sure as hell not." Beth stepped out from behind the pillar, pushing back the hood of the Robe. "Sorry, baby. I dunno why we were hiding in the first place, once we knew who these folks were." She gestured around the room.

"These are probably the best minds on the planet to help you do what you want to do."

"Indeed," said the Cook. "The Keepers of the Archive will help you summon your good King, as prophesied. Though I would say any King who kills Goromath and Apraxos is a good one."

Aleck dropped his act. "Even if he kills innocent people in the process?"

The Cook smiled. "These Keepers share your concern for preserving life. They hold that everyone is redeemable, even within the span of a single lifetime." He paused. "Even a *Herax*, some of them claim. A view which I do not share." He looked around at the Keepers, then back at Aleck. "I believe a Herax is best redeemed by sending it into its next life. As for the Normals and Shallows," he shrugged, "soldiers are not the only purveyors of harm."

"Okay, okay," said Aleck. "I admit, you guys are the best allies I could have. But here's the thing. Wouldn't that have been obvious to the Master Summoner I saw when I was a boy? Whatever he did, it didn't work out. So maybe teaming up with you-all is the first thing in a chain of events that—somehow—leads straight to those massacres I saw." *And my own fucking death.*

"So you have actually seen the future?" asked the Elder, "not in visions of the Otherworld, but in waking life, with waking eyes?"

"Yes," said Aleck. "When I was a teenager, I came to Melkhaios, arriving sometime after now. I'm not sure how long, maybe a year from now. I met the Cook." The Cook raised his eyebrows. Aleck nodded. "Yeah. Sometime in your future, you meet me in my past."

The Cook stared at him. Tilted his head to the side.

"Don't believe me?" asked Aleck. "I know you are thirty-seven years old."

The Cook's eyes widened, then narrowed again. "Thirty-six."

"Right. Thirty-six. A year from now, you're going to tell my teenaged self that you're thirty-seven."

"My 'birth day' is tomorrow."

"Whatever," said Aleck. "*Sometime* in the next year."

"What else did you behold then?" asked the Elder.

"I saw the enslaved folk and wild folk rise up together," said Aleck, "and slaughter not only the Herax, but Normals and Shallow Ones—whether combatants or not. They were led by a Cannibal-King who did nothing to stop the massacres." He looked at the Cook. "You helped him."

The Cook looked dispassionately back at him.

Aleck continued. "Then I was cast out of your world against my will, and I've spent my life trying to come back here and undo the harm I helped cause. Now I need to figure out how to perform the summoning correctly. To bring a good Cannibal-King."

"Please, clarify," said the Elder. "If we are to aid you—or avoid aiding you—then we must understand. We have an abundance of scripture, as you see," he gestured around the room at the inscribed pillars, "but even amongst ourselves we disagree as to interpretation. So you say your past self will soon come as our First Herald?"

"Yes," said Aleck. "Like, that line about tilting the Watcher's ships sideways? When I was a kid, I knocked over some Herax ships by ramming their sails with rafts from the Circus."

"Rafts from the Circus?" said the Elder. "But, to do that, you would have to steal the Circomangkus from Apraxos himself!"

"Uh, yeah."

"Hoy, hoy!" said the Keepers.

"Boum!" bellowed the Cook.

"Boum!" echoed a few Keepers.

The Elder bowed his head. "Master Summoner, we are at your service!" He looked up at Aleck, beaming.

"Okay, okay. We have a year to plan. I'm sorry I was so wary about accepting your help. You promise you'll help me figure out how to summon a Cannibal-King who'll prevent the massacres?"

"Of course!" The Elder laughed. "Master Summoner, your caution is admirable, but I think perhaps your doubt is excessive. It is as though you doubt even yourself!"

"Of course I do."

"Master Summoner, please."

"Call me Aleck. And promise you'll back off, if I think your assistance is interfering somehow with us summoning a just King."

"Of course. Are we agreed on this?" the Elder asked the other Keepers.

"Hoy, hoy," they said, except for a few, who exclaimed, "Boum!"

"Our main concern," said the Elder, "will be interference from the Shallow Ones. It is hard work keeping secrets from them, especially here in the heart of Kaios University. We are surrounded by them and their schemes."

"Sorry," said Aleck, "aren't you—uh—aren't you a Shallow One?"

The Elder frowned, looking insulted. "No."

"You, uh, but you—"

"I have no gill fronds. It is not because I trim them in the fashion of the Shallows. It is because, when I was a boy, a Shallow One tore them out at the roots. This is why I know the importance of protecting the innocent. Long did I dream of killing Shallows, as vengeance for what they did to me. Indeed, I did more than dream. But the truth of vengeance is that every death and injury merely cultivates in our opponents the exact resentment I carried in my heart. Everyone believes himself justified; everyone believes himself to be acting in self-defense; and everyone's suffering is real suffering—even the suffering of a villain. And a villain's suffering feeds his villainy. So everyone who commits an act of revenge sows the seed of vengeance back upon himself. This is as true for the Deeps as it is for the Shallows." He nodded solemnly for a moment. "So, to clarify: nothing would please me more than a bloodless revolution."

"I have a question." Beth slapped the Cook's shoulder with the back of her hand. "How did you know I was back there?"

"I smelled you on him. Your scent was only a few seconds old. So was the scent of your Robe—that's why I thought he smelled like a Keeper."

"But I was wearing the Robe."

"Certainly. I didn't smell you behind the pillar. I just smelled him, and everything on him. The Robe doesn't hide his scents when he's not wearing it, not even its own."

"Oh. And, like, how did you know I was his wife?"

"You are, aren't you?" The Cook quickly sniffed them both. "You mate for life on Earth, do you not? You smell like mates-for-life."

The door burst open. In the doorway stood two figures with bulging eyes and blue-green faces. They wore heavily ornamented robes. No gill-fronds hung from their nose-slits. Behind them stood several more Shallow Ones, wearing only fancy harnesses bristling with weapons.

The Shallow One with the more elaborate robe said, "Who are these trespassers?"

# The Arch-Dean

Aleck froze.

Beth threw the hood of the Keeper Robe over her head.

"Ah, Arch-Dean Werumel," said the Elder. "Welcome to our Council. This is our guest, the Cook of Corpsewater."

The Cook bowed. "And this is my..." he looked at Aleck, "my Assistant Cook."

The Arch-Dean glowered at the Elder. "How dare you defile the precincts of my University with filthy dog-apes from the forest?"

"We have no such prohibitions in the Archive," said the Elder, calmly. "On the contrary, the Archive's charter specifically prohibits exclusion based on species or ethnicity. We have had Wilder Keepers here, long before your time, as I'm sure you have heard."

"Miscegenist! Soon you'll be hosting bloodthirsty Givers!"

"That would not be prohibited by the charter," said the Elder. Stifled laughter rustled among the Keepers of the Archive. Aleck relaxed; the Elder and Arch-Dean must argue like this often. Still, he couldn't ignore the abundance of weapons on the Shallow Ones in the hall.

"Bah!" The Arch-Dean threw his hands up. "Then what would prevent the Givers from turning your precious Archive into a military base? You could host an army of Givers, helping them to attack Melkhaios from within as well as without!" He narrowed his huge eyes and pointed at the Elder. "You are a traitor."

"Hoy hoy," said one of the Keepers, facetiously. Aleck guffawed loudly, then slapped his hand over his mouth.

"Using the Archive as a barracks or base of any sort," said the Elder, "is also prohibited by our charter."

"Damn your charter!" snarled the Arch-Dean.

A few Keepers uttered small gasps—some sarcastic, some genuine.

"Our charter was composed by Kaios himself," said the Elder. "Dishonor it and you discredit the foundations of the entire University."

"Bah! I am Arch-Dean Werumel! This is my University! I dictate what serves it credit or discredit!"

"This is Kaios University," said the Elder, "not Werumel University."

The Keepers of the Archive laughed openly at that.

"What? You insult my rank and station? You insult the office of the Arch-Dean?"

Aleck made an involuntary whistle of surprise at this skid beyond the bounds of logic.

"No," said the Elder. "Not the office."

"Yes!" said the Arch-Dean.

"Wrong." The Elder laughed. "You discredit yourself with your faulty reasoning."

"What? Now you insult my capacity for reason!"

"Dude," Aleck butted in, unable to resist, "you have got to be kidding."

"Silence, dog-ape!"

"He insulted your reasoning, not your capacity for it," said Aleck.

"I said be quiet!" said the Arch-Dean.

"Not that you've shown any sign of capacity, either," said Aleck.

"You impudent cur!" He turned to the Elder. "I want these dog-apes gone from here, never to return. And I expect full atonement for their insults."

"I respectfully decline both requests," said the Elder. "You cannot dictate conduct within the Archive."

"Anarchist!" said the Arch-Dean. He turned to the guards behind him. "Evict the dog-apes, with whatever force is necessary!"

"Shit," said Aleck.

A pair of guards shouldered their way through the door and sidestepped along the wall to make way for another pair, who did likewise, followed by a third pair.

"No!" said the Elder.

The Cook drew forth the Sacred Bone from his belt and laughed.

"Whoa, whoa, whoa." Aleck backed up, bumped into someone, jumped with startlement, and turned to look at a Keeper with her hood up. "Excuse me—uh, 'sister'?"

"Aleck, it's me," said Beth.

He peered at her face, obscured from his awareness by the magic robe. "Me who?"

The Cook rattled the Bone one by one at each of the Shallow Ones, going down the line as he spoke: "Werumel, you are witless to believe eight of you will stare down an ancient, angry Wilder. I could kill eight *Herax*. Eight Shallow Ones?" He laughed again. "I can remember eight centuries before the first Shallow One crawled out of the slime of the bay."

Aleck stifled a chuckle at the Cook's convincing lie, pretending to himself that he wasn't terrified.

"I-i-impudent dog-ape!" The Arch-Dean fumbled in his robes and drew forth a long, thin, one-edged knife and stepped backward.

"Fighting in the Archive is most definitely prohibited!" The Elder got up and walked across the floor, bringing his pillow with him, and sat down in front of the Cook, facing the Arch-Dean. The other Keepers followed suit and sat in a cluster, blocking the floor before the Cook, facing the Shallow Ones.

"I carry the Shinbone of Kaios." The Cook shook it at the Shallow Ones. They froze in awe of it.

"Defiler! You have turned one of the Sacred Bones into a pagan fetish!" With his empty hand the Arch-Dean reached out. "Give it to me! It belongs to the University!" He made an intricate gesture, muttering a momentary incantation— then grasped at the air.

The Shinbone nearly flew from the Cook's grasp; he lurched, then pulled it back. "You won't dominate me with your tame little magic games. If the Shinbone could belong to anyone other than Kaios—"

"Kaios is dead!" said the Arch-Dean.

"—then it would belong in the Archive," continued the Cook.

"Not necessarily," said the other robed Shallow One, from behind the Arch-Dean.

"Yes it would," said the Elder, "although any of the Schools of the University would be free to request it for study."

The Cook handed the Bone to the Elder, who took it reverently. "I offer this to your rightful custody. These beads belong to my people."

"Guard the Bone well, then." The Elder handed the Shinbone back up to the Cook. He nodded at Arch-Dean Werumel. "You may borrow it another time, perhaps."

"Sower of strife!" said the Arch-Dean.

The Cook pointed the Bone at the leftmost Shallow guard. "Would you prefer the knee end," he flipped the Bone in his hand, "or the ankle end?"

"No killing," said the Elder. "No fighting."

"I pledge to fight only in self-defense," said the Cook, ankle end of the Bone still aimed at the leftmost guard. "But if I must fight, there will be killing."

"There will be no fighting in the Archive!" The Elder stood, placed two fingers on the outstretched Bone, and pushed down on it. The Cook frowned and lowered his arm.

"Give me the Bone!" said the Arch-Dean.

Beth strode across the floor and walked directly up to the Arch-Dean, disregarding his knife. Aleck watched her with bewilderment. Rationally, he knew who she was; but with her hood up, the Robe's enchantment kept wiping her from his attention, moment by moment. It took all his strength of mind simply to keep noticing her. The Arch-Dean glanced at her, then looked away from her to the Cook. Opened his mouth to speak; but she lay one finger against his cheek, and turned his head to look at her. "There will be no fighting in the Archive."

The Arch-Dean froze a moment, then jerked away, goggling at her. "I beg your pardon?"

"There is to be no fighting in the Archive," said Beth. "It's the rule."

"Well, yes, of course." The Arch-Dean adjusted his robes. "'Blood ruins books,' as the saying goes." He scrutinized Beth's face. "Do I know you?"

"She is our newest member," said the Elder.

"My name is Beth," she said, bowing slightly.

The Arch-Dean fumblingly sheathed his knife somewhere in his robes. "Well, we'd best be going. I don't have time for this unsavory nonsense." He turned to leave, then back over his shoulder, "I want that Bone! I expect it on my desk tomorrow!" He strode out of the room, followed by the other robed Shallow One. The guards looked at one another in confusion, then backed out of the room, hands warily hovering near their knife-handles. Beth shut the door after them and pushed back her hood.

Aleck looked at her. "The heck just happened?"

"I don't even know, man." Beth leaned against him. "I feel high. Was I possessed?"

Aleck put an arm around her, and with the other he gestured wildly. "You glided across the room like a, like a chess queen, and off he goes!"

The Elder bowed. "My lady, are you a new incarnation of Oshta, teacher of Kaios the Summoner? Your face is identical to hers, though wood-brown instead of sea-green."

"Fucked if I know."

The Elder took Beth's hands and stared into her eyes. "You have what Kaios called, 'the power to clear men's minds,' as Oshta once did."

"Dunno about that, man, just look at my husband."

Aleck made a face.

The Elder persisted. "Surely you are lady Oshta, come to us in a liberated manifestation?"

"Maybe for a second there," said Beth.

"Or you have learned how to incarnate twice at once." The Elder pointed at Aleck. "Using his powers of time travel?"

"Definitely don't think that's it," said Beth.

The Elder peered at her. "You're pretending not to know, in order to test us?"

"Nyet," said Beth.

"She's from Earth," said the Cook. "She smells like the race of the Master Summoner, not like one of our First Dreamers."

"Well, that's unfortunate." The Elder frowned. "We surely could use Oshta's help in this matter. You'll have to go visit her. Only she will know what to do."

"She or Great Akaz," said the Cook.

"Not Akaz," said Beth.

"We need Akaz," said Aleck. "He's the one who knows how to do the summoning. Like of course we can't trust him to care about any massacres, so we have to rein him in, but we need his knowhow." He turned to the Elder. "Where is Oshta?"

"As ever, under the mouth of the river," said the Elder, pointing. To Beth: "And you'd best go soon. Your move against the Arch-Dean was decisive, but blatant. I'm afraid he'll discern, before long, that he was the victim of a trick. Your husband needs a robe. Keeper Sozolorin, you're the right size. Would you consider loaning your robe to the Master Summoner?"

"I—I would be honored." A woman in early middle age stood and pulled off her robe. Beneath it she wore a tunic and pants, with a pouch at her belt. With both hands she reverently passed the robe to Aleck. "Master Summoner, may this robe protect you from the prying eyes of the Watcher."

"Uh, thanks?" Aleck put it on.

"Don't forget this." The Cook handed Aleck the Crow Terminal.

"Right. Thanks." Aleck put it in his shoulder bag.

"One question, before you leave," the Elder said to Beth. "How, in Oshta's name, did you obtain one of our robes? Are they commonplace on Earth?"

"Oh, no," said Beth. "It's Aleck's."

The Elder looked at Aleck. "Master Summoner? You must have obtained it when you were here the first time—oh, my." He gestured toward Aleck and then Beth. "They aren't the same robe...?"

"Oh, no." Aleck pointed at Beth. "The Nymph gave me that one."

"The Nymph...?" said the Elder. "The Nymph of the Shrine of the Nubiles?"

"Yeah," said Aleck. "She lives under the bay near the mouth of the river, too, right? Does she live with your, uh, goddess, Oshta?"

The Elder smiled. "Indeed."

"So," said Aleck, "you gonna give us directions, or what?"

"Yes," smiled the Elder. "Come."

"What about you?" Aleck asked the Cook. "You coming, too? That Dean and his minions want to kill you, man."

"Yes. It would be my honor to escort you, Master Summoner." The Cook handed the Sacred Bone to Aleck. "Would you carry this?"

"Uh...sure? Don't you need a Keeper's Robe, too, or something?" Aleck put the Shinbone in his bag.

The Cook turned into a crow and flew onto Aleck's shoulder, leaving his pants lying on the floor. "No."

# The Prayer to the Nymph

The Elder Keeper asked them to put their hoods up. He led them down halls and stairways of an architectural style identical to Aleck's Archive, but in a totally unfamiliar layout. Several niches along the way contained statues of robed figures, none Aleck recognized. At last they arrived at a heavy wooden door, bound in rusty iron; the Elder unlatched it and pulled it open. A heavy, oceanic salt-smell wafted in.

Beyond the doorway lay a cobblestone street, blanketed in hazy murk. Aleck saw clearly for perhaps a couple dozen feet, but beyond that, could only barely discern the dim outlines of ornate stone buildings.

"Wait a minute. Are we...." Aleck reached through the doorway, splashing his hand into a wall of water. He pulled it back, dripping. "We are. We're under the bay." He wiped his hand on his robe.

"Of course," said the Elder. "This is the ground floor. At high tide only the Chamber of the Pillars, where we met you, rises above the waves. Even at the lowest point of low tide, most of our tower remains submerged."

"Why is the water just hanging there in the doorway?" asked Beth.

"The Archivist keeps it out of the tower in which we keep our Archive. Otherwise, our books and scrolls would be soaked."

Beth laughed. "Not what I meant by 'why.'"

"Who is your Archivist?" asked Aleck.

"He resides in our deepest sub-basement, where few have ever seen Him. Before the Great Breach, He was scribe and mentor to Three-Eyed Lady Oshta, who in turn taught Kaios the Summoner. Great Thoth now lies dead and dreaming, waiting for the power that can awaken Him."

"And you say he keeps the water out," said Aleck. "Even though he's dead."

"And dreaming," added Beth.

"Yes," said the Elder. "It is His will. Otherwise, most of the contents of our Archive would likely be destroyed."

"You expect us to go out there?" asked Beth, incredulous.

Aleck stared through the doorway, casting his imagination down the underwater street.

"The Prayer to the Nymph will help you," said the Elder. "Repeat after me: *For the Drownder can pray to the Nymph of the Shrine....*"

"'Drownder'?" asked Beth.

"Air-breather. The Prayer will allow you to breathe water. For a time, at least. Now, repeat after me, please...."

"You call air-breathers 'Drownders'?" asked Beth. "How charming."

"I too am a Drownder." The Elder gestured to indicate his lack of gill-fronds.

Aleck saw Beth's aghast expression. Her heartache made his heart hurt.

"Sorry," said Beth. "Sorry. So how long does that Prayer last?"

"Long enough for you to find your way to Oshta, if you proceed directly. Which you must do. Please, now, you must be on your way before the Arch-Dean comes looking for you."

The Elder recited, with Aleck and Beth repeating, hesitantly, line by line:

*For the Drownder can pray to the Nymph of the Shrine*
*And she gives him the strength to breathe water*
*And she, the Dragons' first daughter*
*Will upon him her Victories shine:*
*The gift of the Nymph to the Drownders above,*
*The spiritual act of physical love.*

The murk beyond the door lifted. Aleck could clearly see the cobblestone path, many stones missing, flanked by intricately carved buildings with many tall, peaked windows. The street stretched ahead.

"I can see," said Aleck.

"Indeed. And breathe, you'll find; and move freely through water." The Elder pointed down the street. "This is Babababadalgharagh Street."

"Bababawhathefuck?" asked Beth.

"'Babababadalgharagh,'" answered the Elder. "That is the word for the sound of the Great Breach. Follow this way straight, and it will lead you to Oshta. Take care not to be led astray by the Spiral Ride, which crosses it several times at the far end."

"I walked on the Spiral Ride," said Aleck, "when I was here as a kid."

"Did you meet any of the Deepest?" asked the Elder.

"What are the Deepest?" asked Aleck.

The Elder made a face. "Cook, will you be able to protect them from the Deepest?"

"Probably." The Cook flexed his claws, gently poking into Aleck's shoulder. "They're reasonable folk."

"*We're* reasonable?" asked Beth. "Or the Deepest are?"

"Both," said the Cook.

The Elder chuckled. "Never have I heard Deepest described as 'reasonable.'"

"Wait," said Aleck, trying to look at the Cook. "Don't you need to say the Prayer?"

"Fortunately, some time ago the Nymph granted it to me for life." The Cook launched himself from Aleck's shoulder and flew with a splash through the doorway. He soared down the street and wheeled around, circling over it in the water.

Aleck and Beth looked at each other.

"You first." Beth laughed and gave Aleck a little shove.

Aleck shrugged, screwed shut his eyes, took a deep breath, and stepped into the doorway with a splash. The water felt cool and pleasant. He stood there, half in, half out. Tentatively he opened his eyes, first one, then the other. He waved his arms back and forth through the water, feeling only a fraction of the resistance he expected from past experience in pools and lakes. Startled by the sensation, he jerked back out of the doorway, exhaling explosively. Water dripped loudly onto the stone floor.

"What's wrong?" said Beth, grabbing hold of his arm.

"Feels weird!" Aleck gasped. "The water, that Prayer—it's thicker than air, but too thin for water, it's... eerie. But lovely, in a way."

"The magic simply alters your relationship with water," said the Elder. "The water is normal, and will act normally when you wish it. You can swim: your hand will cup it, your feet will fan it. But you can also walk, like walking into a light wind."

"Did you try to breathe it?" asked Beth.

"Didn't get that far," said Aleck. His eyebrows shot up. "Oh, no!" He tore open his bag and pulled out his notebook, soaked and dripping. "Damn it!" Holding the notebook by its spiral binding, he swung it in disgust and sprayed a gout of water across the wall, then flung the book to the floor with a splat. Holding the mouth of his bag mostly shut, he poured a stream of water from it into the doorway. It hit the vertical surface of the water, making bubbles and ripples. As the stream tapered off, it trailed across the floor.

"Shit," said Beth. "That sucks. Did it ruin whatever you wrote in there?"

"It's a new notebook," said Aleck, rummaging through his bag to see if anything else in there was vulnerable to water. He pulled out a miniature video camera. "Great."

"Just let it dry before you turn it on," said Beth.

"Really?" asked Aleck. "Are you sure?"

"No." Beth looked at the camera. "But I assume so. I mean, the problem is just that the water conducts electricity, right? So it makes a circuit of all the circuits, and they short circuit...you know what I mean. You just gotta make sure it's totally, totally dry."

"Are you sure?" asked Aleck.

"No, I don't know shit about electronics any more than you."

They both looked at the Elder.

"You don't know about electronics, do you," said Aleck.

The Elder peered at the camera. "What is this object?"

"I'd show you," said Aleck, "but if I do it while it's wet, it'll destroy itself." He looked at Beth. "If it's not already destroyed."

"Does it run on tapes?" asked Beth.

"No, it's from long after all that sort of thing," said Aleck. "No tapes, no discs, no cubes, none of that stuff."

"Why's it still so big?" asked Beth.

Aleck shrugged.

"If it's from a post-tape, post-disc era," said Beth, "it should be the size of a lighter, or a dime, or the head of a pin. Where did we get it?"

"It's an old one," said Aleck. "I got it before we met. From this guy. I told you the story a few times, he wanted video of the ghoul at the university?"

"This is the camera you got from the guy who lived under the overpass?" asked Beth.

"Yeah, that guy," said Aleck.

Beth frowned. "The undercover Reality Patrol guy who lived under the overpass?"

Aleck looked at her. "Uh. Yeah."

"What does this object do?" asked the Elder.

"It records the moving image of whatever you point it at," said Aleck.

The Elder gasped. "Amazing! So it is not unlike the Lens of Ka'ak, which remembers everything ever viewed through it?"

"Sure," said Aleck. "Sounds like."

"If you hadn't been in such a damn hurry," said Beth, "you would have put your shit in plastic bags, like you always do."

"Yeah. Thanks."

# Bababadalgharagh Street

The road lay broken and uneven. To either side stood low, crumbling buildings, many of them partly rebuilt with fitted rubble. Cairns of stacked rubble stood in front of most houses. Innumerable chains of shells hung from cairns and buildings alike. Little flags and long ribbons billowed in the current.

Aleck and Beth half-walked, half-swam down the street. The Cook wheeled overhead in crow form. Deep Ones lounged in groups on porches, dressed in ornamented harnesses of fish-hide and shell, bantering and laughing. Voices sounded tinny but clear through the water. No one took particular notice of Aleck and Beth.

Strange spires appeared in the distance. Aleck asked what they were.

"That's the Temple of Fat Man," said the Cook.

"'Fat Man'?"

"The Deep Ones' god. He is buried beneath it, and will awaken when the Cannibal-King comes."

"Is he dead and dreaming too?" asked Beth.

"Most definitely," said the Cook. "I have had the honor of receiving dreams from Him while in rattle trance. Dreams of the very wildest nature."

Aleck and Beth looked at each other.

The street proceeded for several blocks, each different in their details but in general character much like the last. Ornaments varied: crab shells and claws with red pennants, nautilus shells with green, shimmering abalone with black. Now and then someone pointed at the Cook, with a comment such as, "The Nymph does love a good Wilder now and then!" Peals of laughter echoed through the water in response.

The Cook soared down and took hold of the shoulder of Aleck's robe. "Shallow Town coming up on the left. Let me hide under your robe till we cross Division Street."

"Why?" asked Aleck. "They wouldn't be looking for us because of the Arch-Dean, would they? They don't have Herax telepathy magic?"

The Cook laughed. "No. No, nothing like that. They just hate Wilders. Shallow Town is crawling with guards, inside and out, both Shallows and ghoti-birds."

"'Ghoti-birds'?"

"What's a ghoti-bird?" asked Beth.

The Cook laughed again. "Didn't you see any ghoti-birds the last time you were here?"

"Not that I know of," said Aleck.

"You'd remember if you did. I believe you'll start seeing them shortly. Let me under your robe."

"I'd rather not," said Aleck.

"You must." The Cook looked sidewise at Beth. "Either you or your mate."

"Nope," said Beth.

"Well," said the Cook.

Aleck grumbled as he and the Cook worked out a way for his large, sharp-clawed, big-beaked crow-body to fit under the robe. In the end the Cook perched with a foot clutching Aleck's belt, another foot hooked on the lip of his jeans pocket, and its head nestled in his armpit, beak poking down into the sleeve of the robe.

"Comfortable?" asked Aleck.

"Yes, very," came the Cook's muffled voice.

"Fab. That makes one of us."

The Temple of Fat Man loomed closer. Numerous spires of different sizes rose from a low, hulking dome.

"It looks like a melted cathedral."

"Or a few cathedrals melted together," said Beth.

They continued down the street. Soon a high wall appeared ahead on their left. As they approached it, they could see that this wall must surround several city blocks; and unlike the rest of the buildings they had seen outside the Archive, this wall seemed intact. Things swarmed over it.

"I'm guessing those are ghoti-birds." Beth gestured to indicate the swarm. "Do we have to walk so close?"

"Just walk slowly," came the Cook's muffled voice.

"Won't our robes keep anyone from noticing us?" asked Aleck, alarmed.

"Walk slow anyway," said the Cook.

Aleck nervously forced himself to walk at a steady, even pace. He noticed, much more clearly than before, how the broken terrain of the ruined street intensified the awkwardness of walking underwater, and how carrying the pokey, wriggling Cook interfered with his balance. As they neared the wall of Shallow Town, Aleck felt a continuous impulse to keep an eye on the winged silhouettes of the ghoti-birds; his attention darted back and forth between the surface of the street and the creatures circling over the town, and with every step he feared he might stumble. The current kept threatening to pull back his hood. How much of the robe's magic depended on the hood being up? He glanced at Beth. Did she feel as nervous as he did? Knowing her, not likely. Could she sense his anxiety? Probably even through the magic of his robe.

They walked in the shadow of the wall of tightly-fitted stone. Shallow guards, not unlike the Arch-Dean's, stood unmoving at intervals along the battlements, with several of them clustered at each gate. Aleck forced himself to stop looking up at the ghoti-birds. He couldn't rid his mind, however, of the thought of vicious, taloned creatures swooping down upon them en masse and tearing them to shreds. He put one foot in front of the other. The wall continued and continued. He noticed his pace inadvertently quickening, and forced himself to slow down. The current tugged at his hood.

"Almost there," said Beth softly.

A sudden eddy in the current pushed Aleck off balance and tore his hood back. He looked up and saw its cause: the membranous wings of a dinosaur-looking creature, alighting directly in front of him. It stood taller than him on crooked legs with oversized claws like sets of razor-sharp meat hooks. The massive beast looked at him sideways from a hawk-beaked head the size of a horse's.

"WHAT!" squawked the ghoti-bird.

"Oh my god," said Aleck.

"Don't move!" whispered Beth.

"WHAT!" squawked the ghoti-bird again.

"Tell it you're a Keeper," said the Cook.

"I'm a Keeper!" said Aleck.

The ghoti-bird twitched its huge head to the other side. Aleck jumped.

"What!" repeated the ghoti-bird, fixing him with its other eye.

"Keeper!" said Aleck, his voice cracking. "Keeper!"

Aleck felt something tugging at his collar, and jumped again. The ghoti-bird jumped in response to him, and let out a terrifying shriek. Beth finished pulling Aleck's hood back up. The ghoti-bird looked at them, first with one eye, then with the other.

"We're Keepers," said Beth.

The ghoti-bird flapped its wings and swam away.

They nervously walked the remaining length of the Shallow Town wall, crossed Division Street, and entered another Deep One slum. This neighborhood seemed more sparsely populated than the other side of Division, its buildings less decorated and in poorer repair. They saw fewer groups of Deep Ones socializing on porches. Solitary faces peered at them from behind windows.

"Can you come out of there yet?" Aleck asked the Cook.

The Cook struggled his way out from under Aleck's robe, accidentally scratching and pecking him in the process.

"Sorry," he said, alighting on Aleck's shoulder.

"Dammit." Aleck rubbed his side. "That salt water stings like hell."

"Be glad we're in the bay," said the Cook. "Right near the mouth of the river, no less. It's barely salty, compared to seawater."

"My first pick definitely woulda been don't maul me in the first place."

"The Spiral Ride is coming up," said the Cook. "We'll start seeing the False Shrines soon. Careful you don't get tempted by them, either of you, or we'll never get to the Nymph."

"Tempted by what?" Beth asked.

"The Nubiles of the False Shrines gain their nourishment by pleasing others. Just as a plant feeds on sunlight, or a demon feeds on suffering. They change shape according to the desires of those around them. Hence you may see one who embodies a particular fantasy of yours. It may require willpower to resist distraction."

"Don't even think about it," Beth said to Aleck.

"Gimme a break. Anyway, if I saw one, it'd just turn into you."

"Spare me," said Beth, groaning.

"I fear you are both thinking about this," said the Cook, "in the wrong way. You assume you are immune to temptation. That frame of mind is fertile ground for the spells of the Nubiles. It may very well be that neither of you share the proclivities that will be embodied by them on behalf of whoever their current audiences are. But if you discover that you do share them, or if you encounter a Nubile without an existing audience, passing in their vicinity with a premise of immunity is the very thing that makes you vulnerable. Your desire will sneak up on you. You will not notice as it takes hold of you."

"So?" said Aleck. "Then the rest of us just drag the tempted person away."

The Cook laughed with a jagged croaking sound, then spoke in a grave voice. "Assuming *anyone* manages to resist temptation, those still tempted may resist being dragged away. As you say, your first pick is definitely to avoid enthrallment in the first place."

Ahead it seemed another wall crossed their path. As they got closer, they could see it was more like an earthen embankment with a perfectly flat top. It curved slightly away from them to the right and left.

"That reminds me of the Spiral Mounds," said Aleck.

"The what?" asked Beth.

"The man-made ridges flanking the Spiral Ride," said Aleck. "Wilder-made, I mean. The Spiral Ride is the road that curves around Akaz's tavern, where I saw the Herax kill that kid, remember? On either side of the road, I told you, they have these... mounds."

"Mounds," said Beth. "When I hear the word 'mound,' I think of a big pile of dirt."

"Well, yeah, they're piles of dirt" said Aleck. "Except they're long and thin and run alongside the road. Around and around." He gestured ahead. "They look like that. Cook, what is that?"

"That's the Spiral Ride," said the Cook. "The Mounds were built long before the Ride, mind you. But once the Ride was built, it became very magical as well."

"The Mounds are magic?" asked Beth.

"They're among the Wilders' most sacred places," said the Cook. "We built them even before Kaios came to this island. They are in fact why he chose this area as the site for his perfect city."

"Wow, I didn't know that," said Aleck.

"Yes," said the Cook. "Don't cross the Spiral Mounds. That's inviting bad luck enough to last into your next lifetime."

"That's bad," said Beth.

"Yes," said the Cook.

"So that's the Spiral Mounds," said Aleck, pointing, "continuing underwater. I walked along them with Akaz, up on land."

"You walked the Spiral Ride with Akaz?" said the Cook, fluttering his wings.

"Yeah. When I was a kid. I mean, I'm going to do it, from your point of view. A year from now or whenever it is." He remembered Akaz telling him that the Ride was broken—in fact, that he, Aleck, had somehow broken it. He stifled the thought.

"Truly the Master Summoner has come to us," said the Cook, bowing his head. "I am honored."

"Whoa," said Beth. "*Aleck Woad Superstar.*"

"Hey, c'mon, it's not like I asked for this part."

"Fair enough." She curtseyed.

Up ahead a wide tunnel ran through the embankment where Bababadalgharagh Street passed under the Ride. A crowd had gathered there. "What's going on?" asked Aleck.

"That is one of the False Shrines of the Nubiles," said the Cook. "Several of them are situated under the Spiral Ride like that."

"What? What do you mean, 'under the Spiral Ride'?"

"The Spiral Ride runs along the top, there. During the Breach, when the lower half of the city fell, and the bay swept in, the magic of the Ride kept it exactly in place, floating deeply or shallowly in the water depending on the tide. The Ride is nearly as potent as the Mounds themselves. And stubborn."

"Stubborn," said Beth.

"So that's not the Mounds?" asked Aleck. "What happened to the Mounds?"

"That is only their dead remains," said the Cook. "They fell. Then Thresner the Blue took his army of enslaved earth elementals, and forced the Mounds under the road. He found the Ride uncanny, simply hanging unsupported. The power of the lower Mounds was thereby twisted, stolen, and used by Apraxos to trap Three-Eyed Lady Oshta. Akaz paid Thresner for his folly."

Aleck didn't have the heart to tell the Cook that he had met Thresner, who had managed to survive Akaz's punishment. Another thought occurred to him, though. "Wait a minute. It's still bad luck to cross the Mounds, though, right?"

"The Mounds or the Ride," said the Cook. "They are a ritual path, meant to be walked from end to end. Leaving the path partway along it, or crossing it heedlessly...."

"I crossed it," said Aleck. "Back when I was a kid, on the night of the Battle of Melkhaios, I cut across from the *God-Dog* into the city...."

The Cook flew from Aleck's shoulder and alighted on Beth's, eyeing Aleck warily.

"Maybe that's what went wrong!" said Aleck. "That's what jinxed the whole summoning of the Cannibal-King!"

"Sure." Beth's tone caricatured humoring him. "Of course. *That* would do it."

Ignoring her, Aleck reached in his shoulder bag and pulled out his notebook. He froze, stared at it through the water. "Damn it! I need to write that down! Beth, help me remember that!"

"Remember what?"

"I need to make sure my younger self doesn't cross the Mounds!" Aleck stuffed the soaked notebook back into his soaked bag.

"Okay. Don't cross the Mounds. Or the Ride." Beth raised an eyebrow. "Doesn't staying on this road count as crossing?"

"Not if you pass under it," said the crow. "Or if you fly over. Set foot on the Ride, though, and you'd best follow it to the end, in one direction or the other."

"We can swim over, can't we?" said Aleck.

"Look at the height of the water, though." Beth pointed.

"We are near low tide," said the Cook. "With only a wing-span of water above the surface of the Ride. And there will be current in that narrow space. Are you strong swimmers?"

"If it's a matter of bad luck lasting me into my next life-time," said Beth, "I'm not risking it."

"That is wise," said the Cook. "Accidentally touch a finger to the Ride as you pass over, and you have defied the Spiral."

Aleck shrugged. "Well, we're not in a hurry, really, I guess. I'm eager for Oshta's advice, but I reckon we can just swim up there and walk the short end of the Spiral to her, huh?"

"True," said the Cook, "though you should not speak so lightly of it. Walking even a portion of the Spiral is an inner as well as outer path. It can be a trial."

"How so?" asked Beth.

The Cook cocked his head one way, then the other. "What happened when you walked it with Akaz, Master Summoner?"

"Huh?" said Aleck. "What happened, like, spiritually, you mean? Nothing, so far as I know...."

"But what happened?" repeated the Cook.

"Physically?"

"I do not understand your distinction," said the Cook. "fate is fate. What happened on the Ride?"

"Uh..." said Aleck, "well, we saw Apraxos. He had kidnapped some of the Nubiles. And the Herax killed a boy and ate him."

The Cook stared at him.

"What?" asked Aleck.

"You call that 'nothing'?" asked the Cook.

"I dunno," said Aleck. "I guess it's just not the sort of thing I was thinking you meant...."

"It's not the sort of thing I want to deal with if I can avoid it," said Beth, "I'll tell you that much."

"Okay, okay," said Aleck. "Why don't we just circle around alongside? I want to get to Oshta, but we're still not really in a hurry...."

"Oshta is at the heart of the spiral," said the Cook. "If we walk along the spiral at the foot of the Ride, it should have an effect much like the Ride itself."

"Wait," said Beth, "that doesn't make sense. If walking alongside it is the same as walking on top of it, then wouldn't crossing under it be the same as crossing it up top?"

"Perhaps you are right," said the Cook. "And perhaps we should therefore go alongside, rather than through. However," he said, pointing his beak to the right, "the ruins of the Old Market lie in that direction. The Deepest lurk nearby. I wouldn't be surprised if they asked for one of us as payment, for passage of the others."

"Asked for one of us?" asked Beth.

"Yes," said the Cook. "To eat."

"Okay, so we're not going that way," said Aleck.

"Back in the Archive you called them 'reasonable'," said Beth. "That's 'reasonable'? What's 'unreasonable'?"

"Eating us all," said the Cook.

"That leaves going through," said Aleck, pointing ahead. He felt a thrill in spite of himself at the prospect of passing near a False Shrine.

A free-standing arch of fitted rubble stood a few yards out from the mouth of the tunnel. It looked frail. Beside it stood a pair of Shallow One guards with spears and knives.

"Box office," said Aleck.

Beyond the arch, Bababadalgharagh Street continued through the embankment. The Spiral Ride crossed over the break like a concrete overpass back on Earth, the banks sloping up both sides, the Ride's cobblestones hanging impossibly in the water. Beneath it huddled a crowd.

"I'll need to hide under your robe again, Master Summoner," said the Cook.

"So you want to go that way?" Aleck asked Beth.

"Sure. It beats watching people eaten alive by Apraxos."

"Herax ate the kid, not Apraxos," said Aleck.

"Whatever," said Beth. "And it beats getting eaten alive by these Deepest, whatever they are. All we have to do here is pass unnoticed through a crowd, right? Wearing magic robes. And they couldn't care less about us anyway, they're kinda busy. Piece of cake."

"But what if passing under the Spiral Ride counts as crossing it?"

"Hmm. But what if we second-guess everything, every step of the way?"

"The massacres I witnessed as a kid were caused by people not second-guessing enough."

"No they weren't. They were caused by mobs of blood-thirsty jerks in a frenzy. You already have bad luck clear through your next lifetime from crossing the Spiral Ride when you were a kid, right? Who cares if you cross it again?"

"My luck could get twice as bad, for all I know!"

"Christ. The only bad luck that would come of walking under that thing would be if the street fell on you. And since it stayed put through an earthquake that sank half the city, I don't think we need to worry about that!"

"Just gimme a minute to think, okay? What's the rush?"

The Cook squawked and flapped his wings, looking back the way they came.

Beth turned. "There's the Arch-Dean."

"Shitfire." Aleck looked back over his shoulder. The Arch-Dean and his henchmen approached, half a block away. The guards carried spears. Aleck hurriedly bundled the Cook under his robe, getting more scratches in the process.

"Come on." Beth took Aleck by the arm and led him out of the street into nearby ruins. They huddled beside a crumbling wall, one story high and several yards wide. Words and numbers had been crudely scratched into every inch of the stone surface. Aleck realized they must be names and dates: graffiti signatures of proud visitors to the False Shrines.

"They probably saw us," said Beth. "I think we're gonna get a chance to test how strong the magic is in these robes."

"We can't bank on them." Aleck moved to the edge of the wall furthest from the street, and pointed with a zigzag gesture. "Let's make our way up to that crowd, doing our best to stick to rubble that that keeps us hid from both the box office and the Arch-Dean's posse."

"You go first," said Beth.

"Any objections, Cook?" asked Aleck.

"No!" croaked the Cook. "Go!"

"Let's go!" said Beth.

Aleck sidled around the corner, striding leisurely to the next section of crumbling wall and squatting beside it. He peered around one end of it: he could see the street, but not the Arch-Dean. The only sound came from the crowd of men under the Spiral ride. Aleck heard occasional cheers, tinnily muffled by the water, and a constant murmur that sounded like a stew of varied moaning. Aleck looked around the other end of the wall and saw the stone "box office" archway with its two guards. They seemed immersed in conversation; at least they hadn't noticed him and Beth. The Arch-Dean and his crew knew what they were looking for, though, and might have magical assistance to counter the robes. Aleck and Beth needed to get into that crowd and out the other side. Then there would be another two or three more tunnels under the Spiral Ride, presumably with more False Shrines and crowds of men. Aleck didn't like the idea of having to repeat this process. Crowds, though, between them and the Arch-Dean, would give them a good lead....

Beth walked up and squatted beside Aleck. "These ruins give us good cover. Walls overlap from any vantage point."

"Sh!" said the Cook, from within Aleck's robe.

"Did you see the Arch-Dean?" whispered Aleck.

"Corner of my eye. Just for a fraction of a second, through the gap between two walls. They didn't see me."

"You're sure?"

"Babe," said Beth, "how long have we been sneaking around together?"

"Sh!" repeated the Cook.

"Impossible to know," said Aleck, ignoring him. "We've never stayed in one time stream for longer than a year or so."

"Guess."

"I'd say we're in our thirties," said Aleck. "Though, honestly, I feel older."

"Well I'd say we've been doing this maybe twenty years."

"Okay, sure. So?"

"In twenty years," asked Beth, "how many times have I been spotted when I thought I hadn't been?"

"I don't know. A few."

"Not counting times when you gave us away," said Beth.

"I don't know." Aleck pondered. "Not many."

"None," said Beth. "It's always you knocking something over or poking your head out. Or just walking out into plain view like a space cadet, like today."

"What about the revenant?"

"Which revenant?" asked Beth.

"The one in England."

"In the barrow?"

"No, no, Victorian England," said Aleck. "In the house."

"That was you. With your digital alarm watch, remember?"

"Whatever," said Aleck. "I still bet it's more than 'none.'"

"Well nobody saw me this goddamn time!" said Beth.

"Okay okay. We've got to move if we're going to get ahead of them and into that crowd." He crept to the edge of the crumbling wall, peered around, and scampered to the next ruined building. Scratched names and dates also covered this wall.

Beth joined him.

"The hardest part," said Aleck, "is balancing staying hidden versus looking nonchalant."

"How do you mean."

"I don't know how much to trust the robes. What if the Arch-Dean and them can see through the magic? So I want to keep hidden, robe or no robe. But do the robes keep you inconspicuous if you're ducking and crawling and dancing around like a freak?"

"Hard to say." Beth leapfrogged past him and sidled low up to the next wall. He followed. They could hear the Arch-Dean's voice now, pontificating to his group. They couldn't make out his words, but his tone sounded angry enough. Beth led the way to the next ruined building and quickly rounded the corner, getting a firm lead on the Arch-Dean and drawing close to the guards and the box office.

"If we can get to that last piece of wall," Aleck pointed, "we might be able to cut behind the guards without them seeing us." Aleck peeked and saw the guards looking up from their conversation to observe the approach of the Arch-Dean and his crew. Aleck nodded to Beth, then walked with an unassuming stride toward a still-standing house corner: tall, narrow spans of wall meeting in a right angle and rising near the box office like an obelisk. Peering out from his hood, he saw the box office and the Arch-Dean's gang, much closer than expected. Walking across this space felt much more exposed than he thought it would. He forced himself not to hurry, but once hidden in the house corner Aleck sighed a gout of water. He fell into a deep slouch, clutching the Cook tightly. He listened to the arguing Shallow Ones.

"...Preposterous," came the sneer of the Arch-Dean. "You insult not only me, but the honor of the Athwart School itself, and indeed all Kaios University."

"Look, it's simple," drawled the voice of one of the box office guards. "If you don't pay, you can't go in."

Beth arrived beside Aleck behind the house-corner. Aleck gave her a pleading look, hoping for reassurance that she hadn't been seen. She shrugged. He rolled his eyes and slumped back against the house-corner. She put her hand on his arm and whispered, almost silently, "Don't worry. Let's just go for it."

"Sh!" said the Cook very quietly from under Aleck's robe.

"Sorry!" mouthed Beth, shooting a dirty look at the crow-shaped lump in Aleck's robe.

Aleck nodded with a tight-lipped half-smile. He pushed away from the house-corner. His balance wavered, and it took him a confused moment to realize why:

The wall had moved under his hand as he pushed against it.

He turned in panic, and Beth, noticing him, followed suit, her eyes widening. They watched as the house-corner slowly, slowly toppled away from them, the spire of ruined wall falling directly toward the box office.

Aleck wondered whether it moved so languidly because he was frozen in panic, or if the water actually eased its fall. He observed it crumbling gradually across the length of broken pavement. At first it didn't look tall enough to reach, but eventually the topmost stone solidly hit the bottom of the box office arch and dislodged it.

The arch fell, and Shallow Ones dodged the tumbling stones.

Aleck and Beth found themselves standing in plain view.

Shallow Ones stared at them.

Aleck halfheartedly waved.

"Kill them!" said the Arch-Dean. "We'll interrogate their dead souls!"

The Cook erupted from under Aleck's robe, his black wings spreading as huge as an eagle's, grabbing the lapels of Aleck's robe in his claws. The Cook gave a mighty sweep with his wings and hauled Aleck off his feet. Beth grabbed Aleck's wrist and kicked off. The Cook dragged them through the water toward the first False Shrine. Aleck and Beth swam and ran along as best they could. Aleck's bag dragged in the water, its strap digging into his shoulder.

"Gate-crashers!" said the box office guards, propelling themselves swiftly on wide, webbed feet, brandishing their barbed spears.

"Dog-apes!" said the Arch-Dean's soldiers, close behind the box office guards.

The Cook's enchanted wings heaved, pulling Aleck and Beth down the street toward the False Shrine, barely out of reach of the guards. They kicked off from the ground to avoid being dragged across the bay floor. "Don't touch as we go over!" said the Cook to them over his shoulder.

"No!" said Aleck. "Too risky!"

"They won't dare follow!" said the Cook.

"No!" said Beth, desperately clinging to Aleck's arm with both hands. "Go through!"

"Through the crowd?" said the Cook.

"Up the side!" said Beth.

Aleck agreed with her thinking: if they ran along the sloping wall on one side, they indeed had enough room between the heads of the crowd and the underside of the Spiral Ride.

"No room!" said the Cook.

"Sure there is!" said Aleck.

The Cook shook his head. "You'll see," he said, but dove under the Spiral Ride anyway.

Aleck saw dozens of men huddled under the wide cobblestone road. About half of them were Deep and Shallow Ones, some with gill-fronds, some without; the rest looked more or less human, and their clothes looked better suited to the surface world than to this underwater half of the city. They all stood, knelt, or sat in concentric circles around a woman dancing in the center of the tunnel. Most of the men seemed to be twitching strangely. Entering the tunnel, Aleck had to look away from the crowd to kick against the bank; as he did so, it dawned on him what he'd just seen. He glanced down at the crowd. The woman, with blue-green skin and green-blue hair, danced on a pedestal, completely naked. Most or all of the men were masturbating and trying to hide it. The Nubile, shaped by the minds of the men around her, had immense breasts, each fully the size of her torso, bobbing and swaying as she shook them in the water. Aleck watched, fascinated by the scene, unable to take his eyes off of the Nubile's gargantuan breasts. As absurd as she looked, he couldn't ignore a twinge of arousal. *Am I really that much of a tit freak?* he thought. *Or is she casting some sort of enthrallment spell?* Or he might just be responding to the arousal of the crowd of men, buying into their fascination with the creature their desires had created. His train of thought jolted to a stop as he found himself jerked to the side.

The Cook's outstretched wing had collided with the underside of the Spiral Ride. "Ay!" he shouted, tucking his wings as the impact spun him to the side. He kept his grip on Aleck's robe. Beth kept her grip on Aleck's arm, but, swinging low over the crowd, accidentally punted a large man in the face with her booted foot. The Cook spread his wings again as they all glided out from under the Spiral Ride, and he heaved the Earthlings forward through the water. Aleck and Beth soon sank back toward the ruined surface of Bababadalgharagh Street, where they kicked themselves along with giant steps. Looking back, they saw the Shallow guards swimming over and through the crowd. Some of the crowd, led by the man Beth kicked, joined them in the chase.

Ahead loomed the next curve of the Spiral Ride, pierced by Bababadalgharagh Street, with a crowd of men huddling in the tunnel: another False Shrine. The Shallow Ones had fallen behind them; the tactic had worked: the crowd had slowed down their pursuers. Aleck and Beth leapt on, the Cook's wings scooping great currents of water back at them. Darting glances backward as they approached the next Shrine, they watched the box office guards swiftly gaining on them, spears leveled directly at them.

"This time we go over it!" said the Cook.

Aleck looked at the space over the Spiral Ride. He couldn't tell how much room lay between the road and the bay's slow waves, but it looked very shallow.

"No way!" said Beth, alternately kicking the ground and paddling her booted feet. She looked tired.

Aleck certainly felt tired. "It's too tight!"

Ultimately the Cook acquiesced and ran them up the embankment again to one side of the False Shrine. He folded his wings to keep from hitting them in the narrow space. The three of them continued forward for some distance, Aleck and Beth each paddling furiously with one hand; but their momentum soon gave way to gravity, and they began falling toward the crowd. The men at this False Shrine huddled closer together than those at the previous one, even piling on one another at the center. Aleck thought he glimpsed parts of the blue-green Nubile between the gyrating men's bodies. Aleck and Beth clambered along the side of the tunnel, trying to stay up out of the crowd and away from the fast-approaching Shallow guards, but slowly losing momentum and altitude. Just as they seemed about to land atop the pile of men, the Cook threw his wings open and swept back powerful waves at Aleck and Beth, a cloud of bubbles erupting around them. The Cook's claws dug into Aleck's robe and nearly tore free. Beth's grip tightened on Aleck's arm. They flew on a trajectory up and out, their legs whipping down at the crowd. Aleck's sneaker walloped a devotee across the back of the neck. Beth's boots caught a man in the collarbones, flipping him backwards onto the men behind him. They flew past and looked back to see Shallows and Drownders spilling from the mouth of the second shrine. Above the crowd shot the box office guards, their lances and eyes transfixed, one hunting Aleck, one on Beth. The Drownders loped down the broken street, kicking up a low, rolling cloud of silt. Above them the Shallow Ones cut through the water with their strange dog paddle. The Arch-Dean's half-dozen guards appeared, muscling their way through the school of Shallows with some difficulty.

"Dean's guards don't look so tough," said Beth.

"Not compared to those two, anyways." Aleck pointed with his chin at the box office guards. He felt his voice get lost in the current. He thought Beth said, "What?"

The Wilder-crow dragged the Earthlings toward the next bend of the Spiral Ride. "This is the last one before the real Shrine," said the Cook. "Unless she's changed things."

Aleck and Beth looked back over their shoulders again. They had shot far ahead of the crowd, but the two box office guards gained on them, lances poised, their hypnotically smooth, deceptively slow kicking motion leaving only thin trails of bubbles.

With his free hand Aleck rummaged frantically in his shoulder bag, coming up with the Reality Patrol force-grenade. *If we can get them close enough together, we can trap them in an invisible sphere.* He hit the priming-switch. He'd used these before, a dozen times, but the button felt somehow unfamiliar. He looked down to see the wrong symbol: not a blue arrow, a purple one. His antimagic grenade. *But I hid this thing back at the Archive somewhere I'd never find it!* Long ago he had salvaged it, unused, from the site of a Reality Patrol attack; but he had never intended to use it. He knew its disturbing effects. He had experienced firsthand the ambient spiritual deadness that polluted an area hit by one of these, a deadness that echoed backward and forward in time, waves of antimagic hitting the site even before the grenade's detonation, and recurring there periodically in the future for an unknowable time. He had never felt anything so uncanny.

Aleck clicked the switch to turn it off. The tiny red primer-light stayed on. He stared at it, clicking the button a few more times. *Water got in when I turned it on,* he guessed to himself, *killing the switch so I can't turn it off? Or it's just old and malfunctioning? Please don't blow up please don't blow up please don't blow up—*

He glanced back at the box office guards, swimming in close formation, closing on them.

"I'm going over!" said the Cook.

"No!" said Aleck and Beth together.

As they neared the mouth of the tunnel, the Cook swooped low and then angled sharply upward, heaving Aleck and Beth behind him. Aleck felt his robe start to tear—

The Cook shifted into humanoid form. His body spun out, limply, and the three of them collided as they flew toward the edge of the Spiral Ride. The box office guards closed in upon them.

Aleck glimpsed the Cook's face: he looked sick and dazed. The Cook smashed into the edge of the Spiral Ride, his back hitting it almost lengthwise, and he stopped there. Aleck was swept under; Beth swam over. "Beth, don't touch it!" Aleck tried to say—but found himself unable to speak, or breathe. Suddenly roofed over by cobblestones, Aleck scrambled back the way he came, desperate for air. One of the box office guards lunged at him. The barbed spear caught Aleck full in the stomach and slammed him into the underside of the Spiral Ride.

*Fuck,* came his first thought, *I thought I died way later than this.*

Stunned with agony, Aleck stared down at the guard's huge, blank eyes. Below cheered dozens of men without pants, blue-green of skin; among them, dozens of tan men flailed in alarm, some of them desperately trying to swim. Buried below all the men, Aleck glimpsed a third Nubile, wrists and ankles tied to corroded iron rings set in the stone. She also cheered.

Through the pain, Aleck noticed a distant humming sensation in his hand: the grenade. A deep, resonant pulse swept through the water, leaving Aleck with an instant headache—which, rather than being lost in the pain from the spear in him, simply added to it. The grenade glowed and then disappeared.

Of course: the antimagic grenade had canceled the

Prayer to the Nymph, and canceled the Cook's animal form, its weird effects echoing backward and forward in time.

Narrow beams of pale light shone down into the tunnel and spread into a latticework. The men at the third False Shrine looked up in horror and fled the tunnel, clambering over one another to get out, leaving the bound Nubile behind.

Light bathed the tunnel. Terror swept over the face of the guard impaling Aleck. *At the moment of death,* Aleck wondered for a moment, *is my soul bursting forth to avenge me with smiting fire?* The Shallow-guard slammed him against the ceiling again. Pain burst forth from Aleck's stomach to course through his body. *Definitely not dead,* said a small voice in his mind. *Just the grenade. A very different sort of bad thing.*

A cobblestone dropped a few inches onto the back of Aleck's head, not hitting hard enough to do any real injury, but hard enough to bruise. The guard spearing Aleck huddled under him. Slowly, the stones of the Spiral Ride fell, ancient enchantment shattered by the antimagic grenade. Those above Aleck rested on his back, pushing him down on the spear. He wondered if the blade had hit his spinal cord yet. He wondered if the grenade's effect on the magic of the Spiral Ride was causing other overpasses to collapse, or just this one. He wondered if the other guard was killing Beth now. *Both dying, but dying apart from one another,* Aleck thought, *please, anything but that.*

He watched cobblestones tumble slowly down toward the fleeing crowd. He saw the humanoid Cook, moving superhumanly fast now, breaking the Nubile free of her manacles and dragging her to safety. The stones of the Spiral Ride fell down onto the stones of Bababadalgharagh Street, raising a cloud of silt. Aleck couldn't see anyone crushed underneath them; the crowd had fled. Back on the road, however, dozens of Drownder men thrashed and choked, some of them trying to claw their way to the surface.

The guard tilted Aleck sideways, pouring the stones off of his back. He wondered why he hadn't passed out yet. He wished he would. *Maybe I'm not really hurt all that bad,* he thought. The cloud of blood thickened around him. *Is the spear all the way through me?* he mused. *Or is all this blood from the front?* His drowning body choked and spasmed, grinding the barbs in his guts. He saw the second box office guard approaching. No sign of Beth. Aleck couldn't tell if he saw blood on that guard's spear. The Arch-Dean and his guards treaded water at the edge of the fallen overpass. Aleck felt very tired. *God, if I must die on this stupid world, please let me first summon the Cannibal-King, any fucking Cannibal-King, I don't care how many of these assholes he kills.*

Aleck stared at the guard spearing him. The guard smiled. Beth appeared behind him, drew the stone knife from the guard's belt, and slashed him across the throat. The guard dropped its spear to grab its throat, and she planted the knife in his big, fishy eye. The guard drifted away and sank. As the other box office guard approached, Beth wrenched the spear out of Aleck's belly.

*That* surge of pain exceeded everything so far: worse than the stabbing, the weight of the stones, even the fear of dying alone. He wondered if the spear had missed his spine on the way in, only to cut it on the way out. Aleck sank. He prayed to pass out, but still didn't. *To pass out but not to drown,* thought Aleck, *please, god, I don't want to die on this world! Let Beth kill that bastard and somehow get us out of here!*

The other box office guard charged Beth, spear poised. Beth offered herself as an easy target, then turned aside at the last moment. She grabbed the oncoming spear with one hand and lifted her own spear up under the guard's rib cage. His bulging eyes bugged out wider. She gave the spear a hard shove up toward heart and lungs. His tongue lolled out in a cloud of blood. Beth let go of her spear, holding onto his as it dropped from his dying hand. He drifted away, twitching.

"I'll kill all of you!" screamed Beth, her voice booming out over the crowd.

*Please, please, god,* thought Aleck. Then: *wait, she can talk.* Aleck realized he could breathe again. He looked at the crowd. The Drownders had stopped thrashing. Aleck felt something touch his back. As he spun to see what it was, a wave of calm passed over him. The pain in his body remained; but the fear of the pain, the anger toward the pain, vanished, and Aleck perceived that they had been worse than the pain itself.

Aleck found himself in the arms of the Nymph of the Shrine: Beth's exact duplicate, but with blue-green skin and green-blue hair. Could the two of them be interdimensional cognates? Did the Nymph simply shapeshift to resemble his personal ideal? Or was he just seeing things? His awareness dissolved.

# Interlude in Aleck's Smoking Room II

Clark broke the connection and called the Archivist. *He has departed. The keys, Great Thoth! Where are my keys!*

*You hurry,* came the voice of Thoth.

*No, my Archivist... there is no hurry.* Clark shifted his weight from one foot to the other.

*The four disks,* said Thoth. *These four, around the door beside you: they will be your Keys.*

*But only four, Great Thoth...?* thought Clark. *Shouldn't I have five keys? I mean, shouldn't the Acting Archivist have five keys?*

*You are Provisional Acting Archivist,* said Thoth. *You may come and go as you please. But you do not control the Crow Terminals.*

Clark felt crestfallen. *But without the Crow Terminals, I... I control nothing.*

He felt Thoth nod.

*How long must I remain Provisional Acting Archivist?*

*Until,* replied Thoth, severing the connection.

# Oshta and the Nymph

In his delirium, Aleck sensed his body being dragged slowly through the water. Body dull, mind dull, his guts felt like stone. He focused his eyes. Rocky sand and seaweed rolled past below him.

He forced his head up. Beth and the Nymph carried him toward the very end of the Spiral Ride. Ruins of a fallen building lay scattered around. Three spires stood at the end of the Ride; beneath them, the mouth of a cave. Closer, Aleck realized the spires were impossibly tall cairns of precariously-stacked rubble. *I wonder if those cairns were made before the Breach,* he thought idly, then laughed, painfully, at the daft idea of them remaining upright while this half of the city collapsed under the waves of the bay. He let his head drop. *Then again, for all I know, the Nymph could do that. Precarious cairns,* he thought, or perhaps sang aloud. *Precarious cairns / Upright through an earthquaaaake....*

Beneath him, Aleck saw cracked stones carved with worn bas-reliefs of women. The two living women pulled him through the mouth of the cave under the end of the Spiral Ride. He heard them arguing.

"You've got to be kidding," he heard Beth say.

"I do not understand," said the Nymph.

"You must think I'm crazy," said Beth.

"I believe nothing of the sort," replied the Nymph. "Though perhaps I may begin to."

*What?* thought Aleck.

*"Excuse me?"* Aleck recognized that tone. Beth's temper had reached its end.

"He will die unless I heal him," said the Nymph.

"You stopped his bleeding," said Beth. "You eased his pain. Why don't we leave it at that and let him heal. How about that."

"These are not cures," said the Nymph. "They will not last. He will suffer and may die, or I can use simple magic upon him. Your reluctance is deeply unsound."

Aleck found himself pulled onto a thick bed of sea-moss. They roughly rolled him over onto his back, causing pangs throughout his guts that, mercifully, swiftly passed. He looked around the chamber; it resembled both a chapel and a cave, window-slits running down either side. Dim light slanted in to outline the curved walls and vaulted ceiling. Bare stones of the Spiral Ride, seen from underneath, ran down the peak of the arched room like a spine. Beth and the Nymph leaned over him.

"Aleck," said Beth, glowering. "Was this part of your plan?"

"Eh?" asked Aleck.

"Beth," said the Nymph. "You infer schemes where none could possibly exist. How could he have planned to be nearly killed?"

"What," said Aleck, "are you guys talking about?"

"Okay, you're right, but look, he's mine."

"I am you," said the Nymph. "I am your cognate manifestation native to this world."

"So go be with his cognate manifestation," said Beth, "and leave my man alone!"

The Nymph frowned deeply. "Aleck had two cognates in this world. One is dead. The other is not welcome in my bed."

Beth made sharp gestures. "Not my problem, and you can go to hell if you think I'm going to leave him alone in here with you."

"Alone?" asked the Nymph. "Why would you not stay?"

"Huh?" asked Beth.

"Why would I try to heal your husband without your participation?"

Aleck felt uncertain that he quite understood this correctly, or any other part of their conversation, but his heart seemed to be racing.

"Who better than you to know how to touch him?" The Nymph leaned over Aleck and touched the side of Beth's face. "And have you never wondered how it would feel to lay with yourself?"

Beth drew back, staring at the Nymph. She looked at Aleck. Aleck swallowed and raised his eyebrows.

• •

Aleck lay on his back on the sea-moss, weeping quietly for the death he had averted, for his death still looming somewhere ahead on this trip, and most of all for keeping this horrible secret, still, from Beth. She snoozed beside him. He longed to tell her, but at this point how could he, after hiding it for years? Where to start? The Nymph lay on his other side, whispering to him. His tears melted into the bay.

"Crying is essential," said the Nymph. "She invented it for a purpose."

"What do you mean," sobbed Aleck, "'She'?"

"The Earth Dragon," said the Nymph. "Without crying, the cycles stagnate."

"What cycles?"

"Cycles of the body. Cycles of the world. Your body was nearly killed. If you did not cry, then all that fear would remain in your body. It would freeze your heart, or knot your back, or any of a thousand other symptoms. But now your tears shed that fear and dissolve it away into the water of the whole world."

He felt a little bit of peace at her words. Beth stirred. He felt a flash of inspiration to just blurt out his secret, *Hey baby, so by the way it's not just some innocents who die in that Battle, I kinda do too....* He tried to speak, but his tears had done nothing to unfreeze his tongue.

Beth turned and curled up against him. "How long was I asleep?"

"Dunno," said Aleck.

She stroked his chest. Her hand strayed down to his belly. "Does it hurt at all?"

A faint echo of the pain lingered. "Nope." He felt her face smile against his shoulder.

Aleck remembered the Cannibal-King. "Hey, uh, Nymph."

"Yes, child."

Aleck furrowed his brow, unsure whether he felt comfortable with her calling him that. "We came here to talk to Oshta."

"I am Oshta."

Aleck sat up. "*The* Oshta?"

She laughed. "There is only one."

"O-oh," he said. "I didn't think—I didn't realize you were the same person."

"We are. I am."

"Three-Eyed Lady Oshta." He looked at the crescent-shaped scar on her forehead, and recalled what he saw near the end of his first visit to this world: her third eye open. It had not been the best of moments. He elected not to mention that memory of her upcoming future.

"I have been called that."

"Teacher of Kaios the Summoner."

"He was my third and final apprentice."

Aleck nodded and shook his head. "I didn't think you...." He shrugged. She smiled at him.

"You didn't think," said Beth, "that the goddess of magic would also be a nymph."

"It wasn't my first calling in life," said the Nymph with a smile. "But the transition did come naturally."

# Interlude in Rattle Trance

The Cook knelt naked atop the Shrine and prayed.

*This we never anticipated: the Master Summoner a magus of Haugermath, the summoning of the Cannibal-King a massive chaos rite. Akaz, Akaz, Akaz, bring me guidance. Come see your Broken Spiral.*

The Cook saw a black wolf standing across the way, on a lip of the broken Spiral Ride. Fires blazed in its eye sockets. *"What the fuck!"* Its voice made a ripple in the otherworld, drawing the Cook into the astral realm.

The rattling Shinbone of Kaios echoed in counterpoint to the ongoing aetheric reverberations from the collapse of the overpasses. The Cook saw backwards in time: a blur of Akaz racing out of the *Sign of the God-Dog*, running in agitation down the spiral, halting occasionally to sniff the road and curse aloud. Returning to the present moment, the Cook sensed the Nymph and the Earthlings in the Shrine beneath him, Oshta's soul shining up through the aether like the moon shimmering on water. Across the way, crouching at the edge of a breach ten paces across, Akaz stared bitterly down into the last False Shrine, his astral body a burning shadow.

*Ten paces?* mused a voice in the Cook's mind. *What leads a wild man to counting? Do you now reside in your head?*

The Cook focused on the sound of the rattle. "Evil spirit begone." *What was that voice?* He noticed his heart racing with worry. *Who is that voice of doubt?*

*Oh, dear,* said the voice. *Now even you, wild creature of the woods, have grown susceptible to the very, very urban indulgence of Self-Doubt. What a pity.*

The Cook, recognizing the voice, forced a laugh. "Begone, Apraxos."

"Say not that name!" came the muffled shout of Lady Oshta from below.

"Nymph!" said Akaz.

Akaz's voice resonated across space, the broken edges of the Ride shredding any sound that touched them. Sparks danced jaggedly up and down the length of the road. The Cook watched the wounded magic of the Spirals. His seven senses flooded with the wheezing of the Ride, the bleeding of the Mounds. It was dying. Panic shuddered through his aetheric body, dimming its glittering latticework of subtle energies.

*O poor Cook.* Minister Apraxos chuckled. *Poor tame little Cook, succumbing to such a civilized malady as anxiety.*

The Cook felt his physical face redden as his aetheric body lit up with fires of rage. He focused the fire into his head and belly, then flowed these tiny suns together to meet in his throat. Astral fire roared forth from his aetheric lips: "Where are you, Apraxos?"

The Cook saw the answer to his question, past and present both at once. The broken, dying Spiral Ride no longer proved any obstacle to Apraxos; he had simply walked across it in a straight line, crossing its coils again and again, stalking up and down the rolling Mounds alone and on foot. The Cook felt a mixture of dread and disgust watching Apraxos flaunt the great taboo with impunity.

Simultaneously, the Cook saw Apraxos where he stood right now: at the exact opposite end of the Spiral Ride, on the stoop beside the back door of the *Sign of the God-Dog*. The Cook flung his astral body down the cracked road, spinning through it quick as lightning, right up to Apraxos, suddenly stopping face to face. Apraxos lurched. The Cook gazed in through the eye slits of the smirking mask to see the hideousness behind it. *Did my fiery gaze alarm him?*

If it had, Apraxos recovered swiftly. With a wiggle of his gloved fingers, he disappeared behind the door into the building. The Cook slid his astral body under the door into the *God-Dog's* kitchen. For a brief moment, the Cook stood beside Apraxos in the kitchen, as though about to prepare a snack together. Then the door flew open again, and Apraxos burst through into Corpsewater. A warding gesture froze the astral Cook in place. The door swung shut.

*Corpsewater,* thought the Cook. *Why has he gone there? Is he injured? He could never force the Corpsewater Nymph to heal him.* He felt a pang, then, as of a vague premonition: something horrible was destined to happen. *Something* to do with Apraxos being injured? he thought. *Nay, nothing bad could come of that—I'll injure him myself, given the chance.* Panic gnawed again at the fringes of his awareness. He focused on the sound of the shinbone-rattle.

*He is not injured,* the Cook decided, calming. *I would have smelled his astral blood, his fear and pain. Why then go to Corpsewater?* He forced himself through the keyhole.

He stood beside the Corpsewater pool, tasting the stain of Apraxos on the aether around him. *Why would Apraxos come to Corpsewater?* He sought his trail and followed it out of the village, over the palisade, into the forest. The Cook sensed a child, a terrified child. He looked a few moments into the past and saw Apraxos in Corpsewater, with a flailing child slung under one arm, hauling himself over the spiked wooden palisade.

The Cook's awareness snapped back to the doorway in Corpsewater, and he glanced into the future. Young Aleck, face bloody, stumbled into the pool.

Panic rushed over the Cook, snapping him back to his body atop the Shrine. His flesh tingled. The Shinbone of Kaios lay beside him where he had dropped it. Words flooded his mind.

*The broken Spiral Ride. Apraxos can cross it with impunity. The magic of the Spiral Mounds has also been the source that fuels the spell binding Zebdod into his Well— vile Zebdod, Eater of Children. Apraxos goes to feed him, to free him: Zebdod, Hound of Apraxos. To hunt the young First Herald!*

*The First Herald.*

*If Zebdod catches the First Herald, then there will be no Master Summoner: he will have died as a boy. No Summoner to summon the Cannibal-King: no Cannibal-King. Akaz, Akaz, Akaz, show us what we must do!*

The Cook looked. The wolf had jumped down to the Shrine below. The Cook followed suit. "Great Akaz! We must hurry!"

# The Wolf of Kaios

From outside came the unmistakable voice of Akaz: *"What the fuck!"*

Aleck jolted up, a ghost pain pulsing in his abdomen. Beth and the Nymph both lifted their heads and gazed in the direction of Akaz's voice. Across the way, at the foot of the fallen Ride, a large black animal dropped into view. With another bound it landed in the doorway to the Shrine. Its bulk blocked most of the view outside.

"Nymph?" came its rumbling, inhumanly deep voice.

"Akaz," said the Nymph, glowering.

Akaz sat back on his haunches. He still filled the doorway. His eyes burned with flame, undimmed even underwater; the water above his head shimmered with the heat. Bubbles of smoke drifted up from his mouth as he spoke. "The Ride's broken."

"Yes," she said.

Akaz continued. "The magic of the Spiral Mounds, it's hemorrhaging. The enchantment could unravel completely."

Beth rubbed sleep from her eyes. "Akaz?"

"Yep," said Aleck. Still listening, he lay back and stared at the ceiling, tracing the lines and surfaces with his gaze.

"I didn't know your Nubiles could change color," said Akaz.

"She is not of the Nubiles," said the Nymph

Beth laughed. "At my age, I believe the word is 'voluptuous,' not 'nubile.' Long time no see, Akaz."

"Excuse me?" asked Akaz.

"You know him?" asked the Nymph.

"Sure," said Beth.

"Who are you?" Akaz had a faint but terrifying edge of hostility in his voice. "If she's not a Nubile, who is she?"

"I'm from Earth," said Beth.

The Nymph said, "She's my cognate."

"Great," said Akaz. "Which Earth you from, then?"

"Come on, Akaz," said Beth. "You really don't remember me?"

Aleck closed his eyes and spoke into the room. "Your past must be in his future."

"All those years I spent with that dumb dog," Beth said, "haven't happened yet from his perspective."

"Shit," said Akaz. "I don't like the sound of this."

*"We know stuff about you you don't know,"* taunted Beth in a singsong.

"First the Spiral Ride falls," said Akaz, "now you guys show up from offworld. Not only offworld, but from my potential future. This is starting to smell like a path paved with very, very bad luck."

"Please, then, feel free to leave," said the Nymph.

"Don't mind if I do."

Aleck looked up to see Akaz backing out of the doorway. "No!" said Beth.

Akaz froze. He tried to jerk his body away, but seemed unable to withdraw any further. His fiery eyes glanced around in a moment of wild panic, then fixed themselves on Beth. He started to growl at her, a snarl forming on his lips, a deep, croaking rumble slowly accelerating in the depths of his throat.

"Quiet!" said Beth. Akaz's growl stopped. "Down!" she said. Akaz's forequarters buckled, and his huge barrel of a torso thumped to the stone floor, trailing a cascade of bubbles. His flaming eye sockets went wide.

The Nymph leaned forward to better stare at Beth, her eyes also wide with astonishment. Beth sat up fully, pulling in her feet. "Snooze," she ordered, tracing a line with her finger from Akaz's forepaws to the spot where her feet had been. Akaz lowered his head slowly to the floor, glowering with his glowing eyes all the while. He curled his lip to show his teeth.

"Beth," said the Nymph, "you have power such as was taken from me centuries ago."

Beth shrugged. "Dog training is easy. You just have to be consistent."

"How—" said Akaz.

Beth reached forward and scratched Akaz on the top of the head. "You don't remember being the Ali family dog?"

Akaz didn't reply, responding only with a scowl. He turned his scowl to Aleck.

Aleck shrugged.

"Ohlone City, California?" asked Beth. "Mr. Omar Ali, Mrs. Shekinah Ali," said Beth, "and their three daughters, Beth, Magdalena, and Fatima?"

"Doesn't ring a bell." Akaz lifted his head a few inches.

"Hey." Beth pointed at him. "Snooze." He lowered his head once more. "I taught you that one. I came up with that." She smiled. "You're so cute when you lie like that."

"If you don't meet him till his future," said Aleck, "then you haven't taught him that yet."

Beth shrugged at Aleck, then looked back at Akaz. "Sit," she said. Akaz lifted his head and sat up. "Good boy. Down."

Akaz lay back down. "Goddammit," he grumbled.

"Good boy," said Beth.

"Don't screw around." Aleck put his hand on Beth's arm. "He's right. Things are getting crazy, probability-wise. You and him being out of time-sync can't be helping."

"So pretend it's not happening?" Beth laughed.

"No I mean we don't do ourselves any good by amplifying it. You and he start building up a bad resonance between you, it's going to start manifesting as bad luck."

"Speaking of bad resonances," said Akaz, "how did the goddamn Ride fall?"

Aleck felt Beth's eyes upon him. He resisted for a long moment, then turned to look at her. She smiled and raised her eyebrows. Aleck turned back to Akaz to find Akaz staring at him. "Uh, that was me." Aleck frowned and meekly waved his hand.

"What?" Akaz jumped to his feet, fire and bubbles exploding from his mouth. He seemed to grow in size, barely able to fit his head and shoulders in the doorway.

"Laydown!" snapped Beth, stabbing her finger toward the ground at Akaz's feet. Akaz's legs trembled. He turned to glare at her. She furrowed her brow at him and growled, "*Now.*"

Akaz lay down, bared his teeth at Beth, then turned to glare at Aleck.

"I hit the Spiral Ride with an anti-magic grenade," said Aleck, sheepishly. "By accident."

Akaz looked aside for a moment, as though lost in thought, then turned his head back to face Aleck. "Where did you get—"

"Reality Patrol," said Aleck.

Akaz's brows shot up. He struggled to rise, turn, or back away, to no avail.

"No, no," said Aleck, "we're not Reality Patrol, don't worry. The grenade was stolen."

Akaz froze. "Stolen."

Aleck shrugged. "Hey, there's no way they can trace it, right? Its detonation erases its own trail in timespace."

"But that doesn't erase the Reality Patrol data banks," said Akaz. "If they had a continuous trace on it, and they *do* that kind of thing, they'd know when and where it went off. That being here and, what, an hour ago."

Aleck shook his head. "No way. That thing was in the Archive for umpteen years. Patrol can't penetrate the Archive, not with sensors, not with soldiers."

Akaz stared at him. "You're not in the goddamn Archive. It didn't detonate in the Archive."

Aleck waved his hand. "Come on, this world is on the other side of the Archive. They can't track us here."

"That's absurd," said Beth. "Sixty-forty the Reality Patrol is the reason we're stranded here."

Aleck pursed his lips. "Sixty-forty against."

"Enough," said the Nymph. "Akaz, why do you come to my Shrine uninvited?"

Akaz shrank to the size of an English Mastiff and gestured at Aleck with his snout. "Dude here just destroyed the Spiral Ride!" He looked back over his shoulder. "I've been walking the Spiral, trying to preserve its magic as best I can. It's not in good shape, though." He glowered at Aleck. "Why did you break my spiral?"

Aleck winced. "I told you, it was an accident."

Akaz shook his head. "Broken Spiral Ride was bad enough. Now I've got bad luck layered on bad luck. Reality Patrol. Stolen. Accident." He sniffed the water in Aleck's direction. "Weird Luck, all right." He sniffed toward Beth. "You too," he said. He sniffed in the Nymph's direction. She frowned at him. He looked away.

"Well, it's good you're here, I guess," said Beth.

"How so," said Akaz with a grunt.

"We're trying to decide whether to summon the Cannibal-King or not," said Beth. "That's why we're here. We came to ask Oshta."

"What?" said Akaz, cocking his ears back.

"What did you say?" asked the Nymph. "You are the Master Summoner?"

"That's why we were on our way here in the first place," said Aleck, "when I was so rudely stabbed in the guts." He peeked over to find Akaz staring at him. "The Elder Keeper at the Archive told us to come ask your advice about whether to do this thing or not."

Akaz's eyes blazed. "You're here to summon the Cannibal-King?"

"Well," said Aleck, "yeah."

"Or not summon him," said Beth.

"But no, that can't be," said Akaz. "None of the Heralds have shown up yet."

"That's not true," said Aleck. "The Cook's outside. He's the Third Herald."

"I know that," said Akaz. "But his heraldic nature hasn't manifested yet. That part of the prophecy hasn't started yet!"

"Yeah it has," said Aleck. "Starting today. The Cook and the Elder agreed there was a temporal inversion between me as Master Summoner and me as First Herald."

"What?" asked Akaz. "What do you mean, you 'as First Herald'?"

"I'm the First Herald, too," said Aleck. "Was. Will be. It's like Beth's deal with you. I met you in my past. A few times. But none of that happened yet, from your current perspective. And I have the same thing with myself."

"You're the First Herald?" asked Akaz.

"My younger self is. Was. Will be. He's due here sometime in our future."

"Jesus fuck a bagpipe," said Akaz. "You can't cross paths with him."

"Well, we did when I was a kid," said Aleck. "I think that's part of what screwed things up. So yeah, I'm aiming for us not to cross paths."

"Wait," said Akaz. "What do you mean, 'screwed things up'?"

"I shouldn't tell you," said Aleck. "I don't want to bias the outcome. I'm trying to create a new past for myself. And a new future for Melkhaios."

Akaz shook his head. "And you want to summon the Cannibal-King."

"Probably," said Aleck.

"Maybe," said Beth.

"But not the way you saw it as a boy. Not 'screwed up.'" Akaz looked at Aleck. "You mean you saw the Cannibal-King's forces defeated?"

"No," said Aleck. "No way, far from it."

"What?" Akaz sat up. "And you want to change this outcome?"

"Hey," said Beth. "Down." Akaz lay down with an annoyed grunt.

"We may not want to summon the Cannibal-King at all," said Aleck.

"Nonsense!" said Akaz. "What kind of Master Summoner are you!?"

The Cook jumped down from atop the Shrine. "Great Akaz!" he said. "We must hurry!"

# The Well of Zebdod

The Cook described his vision. "He simply walked across the Spiral Ride, Great Akaz. He then went through your kitchen, to Corpsewater."

"Corpsewater?" asked Akaz. "What, is he hurt?"

"My cousin would never heal him," said the Nymph.

"Not of her own volition," said Akaz.

The Nymph shot Akaz a dirty look.

"He is not injured," said the Cook. "Even in a vision I would surely have smelled his blood. No; he simply leapt over the palisade with a girl-child under his arm." He looked pointedly at Akaz. "He went north."

"With a girl-child under his arm." Akaz's eyes flashed with flame.

"Yes," said the Cook. "Toward the Well of Zebdod."

Akaz looked at Aleck.

The Cook also looked at Aleck. "Zebdod Child-Eater."

"What the hell is a Zebdod?" asked Beth.

"Zebdod's a monster," said Akaz, "fashioned by Apraxos out of a false Skull of Kaios."

"Zebdod as in the Jawbone of Zebdod?" asked Aleck.

"Jawbone?" asked Akaz.

"You had it when I met you as a kid."

"You met this Zebdod?" asked Beth.

"Nah, just his jawbone."

"Great Akaz trapped Zebdod in a well," said the Cook. "Hundreds of years ago."

"With a spell," said Akaz. "Which was, come to think of it, powered by the Spiral Ride."

"With the Ride now wounded," asked the Cook, "could the blood of just one child could suffice to free Zebdod from its prison?"

"Maybe not just blood," said Akaz, "but blood and soul, sure, maybe."

"Wait," said Aleck. "I remember now, you said 'Old Aleck' got you the Jawbone. But that was *right* before teenage me got here...." Aleck gasped.

"So," said Beth, "sounds like we're starting to overlap time streams."

The Cook nodded, still looking at Aleck. "I saw you," he said. "Just now, in a vision of Corpsewater. I saw you as a boy. I could smell the blood pouring from the cuts on your face."

"No no no you saw the future," said Aleck, "like a year from now. I'm not due here for a year."

"You don't know that," said Beth. "Clark said he didn't know for sure. And why would you believe what he said anyway?" She looked around. "Reality Patrol's probably on its way right now."

Akaz looked at Aleck. "They've never been to Kaios before, though. We're supposedly unfindable, thanks to the Astral Web. Don't tell me you brought the pigs after you?"

"My young self can't be arriving now!" Aleck felt panic rise through his whole body. "We need to plan this out!"

"Chill, baby," said Beth. "So we gotta improvise, as always. You said so yourself."

"But it's too much!"

Beth laughed. "You always did say your old self looked pretty stressed out."

Aleck stared at her, a look of horror on his face.

"Your young self will be here soon," said the Cook, "very soon, and Apraxos has gone to fetch Zebdod."

"If he frees Zebdod," said Akaz, "your kid self is Zebdod-food."

"Can't you protect me?" asked Aleck.

"He'll get you in your dreams," said Akaz. "Not much I can do about that. He'll eat Young Aleck, and there never will be any Old Aleck, 'cause you will have gotten eaten as a kid."

"Off we fuckin' go, then." Beth stood up and began pulling on her jeans, struggling into denim heavy with bay water.

"I need to think," said Aleck hollowly.

"You're going to rip the jawbone off a False Skull of Kaios is what you're gonna do," said Beth, "before it eats your past self and you vanish."

Aleck nodded with distant eyes.

While he and Beth finished dressing, Akaz paced outside. The Cook performed another rattle trance, standing again atop the Shrine. Aleck stared at the floor.

"Summon no one," the Nymph told him. "The solution to all your problems is simple: flow like water. Your fate is a vessel, yet you fight its shape."

"I have to!" said Aleck. "We just have to summon a good Cannibal-King somehow!"

The Nymph sighed. "Who are you to dictate the nature of the Cannibal-King? You are a maker of prophets? The solution, again, could not be simpler: do not summon the Cannibal-King."

"But I can't change my past as much as that," said Aleck. "Who knows what side effects that could have? That's why we need to plan this out!"

"Or hey what if you give yourself a heart attack worrying about summoning the right hoojiewhatsit," said Beth. "Let's go. Zebdod is real enough, and sounds like he'll have the side effect of you getting eaten as a teenager. So any other bullshit can queue up after that."

"Go," said the Nymph. "Protect your younger self. But do not let Akaz draw you into his schemes. You need not summon anyone."

Aleck shook his head.

"Come on," said Beth.

• •

They hurried through the water walking atop the Spiral Ride, swimming the fallen places across Bababadalgharagh. They saw no sign of any Nubiles or their courtiers. The tide had come in: if Aleck reached up, he could barely break the surface of the water with his hand. He wondered if it got any deeper than this. Sunlight rippled down through the waves. Now and then a current would push him and Beth off balance, threatening to shove them over the side of the Ride. The wolf and Wilder seemed immune. Akaz sniffed ahead.

"You smell his blood," said the Cook.

Akaz looked back at him over his shoulder, nodded almost imperceptibly, then resumed sniffing.

"Whose blood?" asked Aleck.

"Yours," said the Cook. "Your young self."

"No!" said Aleck. "He can't be here yet!"

"He is not," said Akaz. "But the scent of his blood travels backwards in time to us, down along the Ride from the *God-Dog*."

"Future echoes?" asked Aleck.

"Something about the impact of his arrival is sending back precognitive resonances," said Akaz.

"Wait, the *God-Dog?*" asked Beth. "I thought he's supposed to land in Corpsewater."

"He will," said Akaz. "He'll gate into the *God-Dog* from Earth, then right back out another gate from the *God-Dog* to Corpsewater."

"So he just happens to find the right gates, with a concussion and half his face hanging off?" asked Beth.

"Babe." Aleck winced. "Harsh."

"Sorry, sweetie," said Beth, stroking his shoulder.

"His Weird Luck will gain him providence," said the Cook. "But we must hurry. If Zebdod is free when Young Aleck arrives, he will have trouble."

"And we'll have no Master Summoner," said Akaz, "and no Cannibal-King."

"Thanks for not letting us lose track of the real priorities," said Aleck.

"Yeah," said Beth. "Bad dog."

"Whatever," said Akaz.

They hurried on. The road curved around. As they swam the last break, crossing above a rubble-strewn false shrine, Aleck found himself glancing around for the Nubile with absurdly huge breasts. *Man*, he thought, *is her spell still working, trying to enthrall me?* He forced his gaze forward. *I wonder if she even still looks like that, without men around forcing her into that shape.* He found himself glancing around again. Out of the nearby ruins came Shallow Ones with spears.

"What the—?" said Akaz.

"I feared we would see them again," said the Cook. He handed Aleck the Shinbone of Kaios, turned into a crow and soared ahead.

Aleck put the Shinbone into his bag. He saw two dozen, three dozen, four dozen Shallow Ones armed with spears and swimming fast. Behind them came Arch-Dean Werumel.

"Hurry!" Beth grabbed Aleck's wrist and broke into a run. He lurched after.

"You'll never outrun them," said Akaz, pacing them. He opened his mouth as wide as a bathtub. "Hop in." His voice sounded normal, though his mouth didn't move. His eyes burned as large as campfires.

"What?" asked Beth. Akaz cut them off, his mouth gaping before them and growing bigger. Heat emanated from it, and in the water they could smell burnt meat. Little flames flickered along his teeth and tongue. His mouth opened as wide as a doorway.

The Cook circled around and flew in. Aleck looked around at the swarming Shallow Ones. Thrown spears clattered to the stones beside him and Beth. A spear flew straight at Akaz, but upon reaching him it turned in place with a halo of bubbles and sped back toward its owner. The Shallow One tried to dodge aside, but his spear followed him and pierced him through the waist. He sank, squirming, trailing a red cloud.

Beth dove into Akaz's mouth. Aleck hesitated, looked around again. More spears came toward him. He grabbed ahold of Akaz's fangs and clambered in.

Aleck found himself floating in air. Hot, dry darkness. Through a jagged hole in the dark he could see the Spiral Ride. After a moment he realized he was looking out through Akaz's fanged mouth. He looked around for Beth. Not enough light came in for him to see her, or anything. "Beth?"

"I'm right here," came her voice from beside him. They grabbed each other's hands.

Akaz snarled and barked, his voice reverberating so loud that it stunned the humans inside him. His body lurched. Some part of him knocked into them and sent them sprawling across his hollow interior. His jaws snapped shut and they heard a cracking, ripping sound. Something wet flew in and bumped into them.

"Akaz!" said Aleck. "You can't harm them! What about Apraxos's shield!"

Akaz laughed, his voice ringing hollowly. "Apraxos hates Werumel. I can do whatever I want to them." He snatched another Shallow, whose scream echoed deafeningly in this strange space within the wolf and then ceased. Something heavy, wet, and slimy smashed into Aleck and knocked him aside.

A misty light appeared and grew, coalescing into the form of a Shallow One. Its smoky form writhed in terror, its face contorting with pain. The dim illumination cast by the figure revealed a dry, hollow cave full of floating things: Aleck; Beth; the crow-Cook; a bloody Shallow One arm; and the top half of a Shallow One, arms intact, guts streaming everywhere, its soul emanating from it. The Shallow One's soul glowed yellow and caught fire. Akaz hacked, sucking the burning soul up into his throat, where it spun into a whirling fireball. It glowed brighter, hotter. Akaz spat it out past them as a blast of roaring white flame. The bay-water boiled, searing a number of screaming Shallow Ones. Akaz snatched another in his jaws and gulped down its soul, spinning another blazing fireball in his throat, spitting another curtain of underwater fire. As Akaz barked with rage, chasing after fleeing Shallows, Aleck could see poached corpses out through his mouth.

"Fun," Akaz chuckled to himself, his voice rumbling inside him. "Fun times ahead." The half-Shallow and the bitten-off arm floated in the darkness.

••

Aleck and Beth sat to either side of the Ostler, overseer of the local "inn" and hence de facto "mayor" of the village of Corpsewater. All three sat at the long table. The people of

Corpsewater sat at the table and on the lawn around. Fires burned in braziers set on tripods at either end of the table.

Alongside the table and looming over it sprawled the long wooden walls of the building Aleck remembered from his youth as the *Sign of Death's Door*. Behind the building and palisade, forest led up onto a blue ridge. Beyond, the evening sky glowed a peaceful electric blue. The first stars sparked dimly on the horizon.

Akaz circled the village, sniffing at the palisade of sharpened sapling-trunks. The Cook had set off into the woods with the Shinbone; "He'll be but a moment," said the Ostler.

The crowd had gathered swiftly; the people of Corpsewater remembered Zebdod in old songs and fables. None of them were happy to hear of his imminent release. The stolen girl's parents mourned in private for now, but were expected to join the vigil soon.

"Where the hell is the Cook?" asked Beth.

"Found it!" Akaz bounded around the side of the Inn. "Come on!" He lightly sprang over the twelve-foot palisade. His voice rumbled outside the wall: "Where the hell is the Cook?"

"Well, I guess it's time to go," said Aleck. He and Beth got up and began making their way through the crowd. People looked up at them with sad faces. "Look, don't worry," he said. "We're gonna get him, I know it."

"You are going to kill him?" asked a boy.

"Aleck is gonna rip Zebdod's jawbone off and whack him with it," said Beth, pantomiming. A few people laughed.

"And then the First Herald is coming," said Aleck flatly. "And the Cannibal-King." He felt no enthusiasm. *And for me, the grim reaper.* The crowd stirred, however, at his news.

"You know this?" asked the Ostler, astonished.

"I'm pretty sure," said Aleck. "Look, we gotta go." He and Beth made their way toward the palisade gate. The Ostler trundled along after them

Akaz came in the gate, irritable. "Look, what's the holdup?"

"Great Akaz!" The Ostler knelt. "I know not how you can dare help us. For Apraxos knows the Rites of Haugermath; his false Sovereign Shield defends him against you and Oshta. Anything you do to him will turn against you."

"So I won't do anything to him," said Akaz.

"We will come with you and fight," said the Ostler, "every man, woman, and child."

"Wrong," said Akaz. "Look, just keep your people here. You'd be throwing your lives away, you know that. The song 'Zebbo Child-Bender' is true. He killed almost everyone in Corpsewater, way back whenever it was, before the Great Breach. Your Nymph almost died trying to heal the survivors."

The Ostler bowed his head. Many in the crowd grumbled; others shushed them.

"Stay inside the palisade, all of you," said Akaz. "And watch your children. Lock them away. If he gets the chance, Zebdod will turn them into fiends and send them against you. And by fiends I mean bent into something truly fucked up, worse than in the song." He left. Aleck and Beth followed him; at the palisade gate they awkwardly waved goodbye.

They circled around the outside of the village toward the wooded ridge. The Cook appeared. In one hand he held a bow and a few stone-tipped arrows; in the other, the Shinbone.

••

Aleck and Beth followed Akaz and the Cook through the darkening woods. The gentle wind sounded like sinister whispers in the trees. They marched up a slope carpeted with leaves and needles, Aleck struggling to walk quietly on the slippery surface. A row of smooth boulders ran along the thinly-forested ridge crest, stretching for an unknown distance in either direction like a path of giant stepping-stones. Aleck saw an explosion of magenta cloud crossing the western part of the sky. Stars in darkness brimmed at the opposite horizon.

Akaz kept his nose to the ground as they descended the other side of ridge. He sniffed back and forth at a narrow cave mouth. "He's still in there," Akaz said in a hoarse whisper. "No tracks coming out."

"No Zebdod tracks, either?" asked the Cook quietly, holding an arrow to his bowstring.

"No," said Akaz. "They're both inside." Turning to Aleck and Beth, he tripled in size, opening his mouth so wide that Aleck feared he would fall in. "Hop in. You're not safe anymore."

"I don't think so!" said Aleck. "Last time I didn't like it too much in there." A hot wind engulfed him, thick with the savor of burned meat. Akaz grunted in annoyance, snatched Aleck and Beth up into his mouth one by one, swallowing them whole. The gory Shallow-parts were gone from Akaz's insides, but the smell of burnt fish-grease remained.

"Keep this safe," came the Cook's voice. Something flew in through Akaz's mouth and hit Aleck on the head.

"Ow!" The object was hard, heavy, and made a rattling sound when it hit him. It floated near him, glistening: the golden shinbone, wrapped in spiral strands of wolf tooth beads.

"You got that?" Akaz's voice rumbled everywhere.

"Yeah." Aleck tucked the Shinbone of Kaios into his belt.

"I'll go have a peek at what they're up to," said Akaz. Out through his mouth, by the firelight of Akaz's eyes, Aleck could see the cave walls. Akaz looked down. A circular pit yawned in the floor ahead of them. Akaz dove in.

They landed with a jolt. Aleck saw a patch of unworked stone floor, but the light from Akaz's eyes didn't reach the walls. *Assuming there even are walls in the Well of Zebdod,* thought Aleck—then, *aww, man, why do I have to think things like that?*

"Where's the girl?" asked Beth.

Light moved in the darkness. Through the space between Akaz's snarling jaws, they could see a glowing human skull walking on four taloned legs.

"Welp," said Akaz, "she's dead."

The thing circled around them with its spiderlike gait, its wicked claws clicking on the stone floor. Sound emanated from it: an eerie voice, like a chorus of small voices, singing.

*Zebdod, Zebdod seeks you now*
*Coming from the old Well*
*Master hunts for Herald*
*Hellhound cannot save you, can't you see*
*Zebdod, Zebdod seeks you now*

A silver thread, like a leash, led from the skull-thing to a long-fingered hand in a pale glove. A robed figure stepped into the glow, stooping and yet still ungodly tall, its features concealed by the hanging folds of its robe.

"Well, well," came a voice from the depths of the hood. The figure leaned closer, and through Akaz's mouth they saw the bottom half of a smirking white mask. "Akaz, are you behind all this? I should have known." Aleck recognized the voice immediately.

"Hi," said Akaz. "Behind all what?"

"'Nobody likes a bad doggie,' as the saying goes," said Minister Apraxos. "There is a proper order to things. If you understood that, if you really understood your role in this world, you wouldn't cause yourself such trouble."

"Some kinds of order are real," said Akaz, "and some are just made up. And Apraxos, m'boy, you've always been one of those people who can't seem to tell the difference."

Apraxos tilted his head to the side. "On the contrary. You seem to be the one overlooking the patterns inherent to this situation."

"Oh?" said Akaz. Aleck and Beth's floating bodies shifted as Akaz sat down. "I have time for a lecture. Explain."

"Have you come to kill young Zebdod?" asked Apraxos. "That would be exciting, to be sure." The glowing skull clacked its jaws and pranced with clicking claws upon the stone floor. "Have you forgotten that I incubated Zebdod here, four hundred years ago, in the Skull of your dead old master, Kaios Spirit-Tamer?"

"I wish you'd quit calling him that crappy name. Kaios never tamed a damn thing. 'Wildness is the essence of life,' even."

"And so, since I created Zebdod," continued Apraxos, "he is protected by my Sovereign Shield. Anything you do to him will turn back against you in some fashion."

"Look," said Akaz, "sorry I didn't knock. I just noticed you were in the neighborhood, so I thought I'd invite you over to my place."

Apraxos ignored him. "Don't you see the tangled lines of fate you've woven? Immediately in the wake of the breaking of your Spiral and my Web, with all the resultant waves: you, the Wolf of Kaios, here with Apraxos and a creature nicknamed the Wolf of Apraxos in mockery of you, sired by Apraxos through the Skull of Kaios? The strands create a Haugermath resonance. You stand against Zebdod, and his creator, in his birthplace; more resonance. Every overlap gives me power." He paused. "Meanwhile your would-be King's alleged Herald floats helpless in limbo, between the shards of the Astral Web and the world of Kaios."

"Well," said Akaz, "there's beer at the Inn, maybe we can find you a straw so you don't have to take your mask off."

"The Rites of HauHaugermath!" said Apraxos, furious. "Everyone remembers Apraxos as Master of Augermath's rites of death magic, but they forget my expertise with the Rites of Haugermath! They forget I can tilt fate itself!"

"You want some stew?" asked Akaz. "We've got some back at the Inn. Or how about some smoked ribs?"

"Akaz, you cretin," said Apraxos, laughing, "you have trapped yourself! If you make a single misstep, here in the Well of Zebdod, you will create such a jangling among the strands of fate, and I will draw so much magical power from the resonance, I'll send tornadoes upon Corpsewater and fling it into the sky! Along with your obnoxious Herald."

Zebdod leaped and capered, singing:

*Zebdod, Zebdod finds you now*
*Herald in the Hellhound's mouth*
*Master catches Herald now*
*Hellhound must spit Herald out*
*Zebdod, Zebdod finds you now*

"What's that you say, Zebdod?" Apraxos stooped lower and peered into Akaz's mouth. Aleck saw the white mask; a chill swept over him as he looked into the bloodshot eyes of Apraxos.

"Akaz!" Apraxos clasped his gloved hands together, causing the silver threadlike leash to slowly whiplash in a wave that flowed down its length. "Splendid! You even bring the Herald with you."

"How does he recognize you?" asked Beth.

Aleck shrugged. "Maybe he saw me when I was in the Astral Web."

"But you were a kid then," said Beth.

"I dunno. Maybe he's looking at my astral body or something." Leaning toward Akaz's mouth, Aleck shouted, "Hey, I ain't no Herald!"

"It is as though you have not only shown me all your cards, Akaz," Apraxos said, "but handed them to me, along with your purse."

"I don't carry a purse," said Akaz.

Apraxos continued beaming. "I don't know when I have last seen such ramifications. Each layer of resonance amplifies the rest!" His entire body tensed for a moment, blue sparks crawling up and down him. "The cosmos," he said hoarsely, "is coiled like a spring here."

"Sure, sure," said Akaz. "A spring. So you're not hungry?"

"Indeed, Akaz," said Apraxos, "even if you take no action that intersects my Shield, I can harvest the discord caused by your mere presence here. You have made a terrible blunder by coming. Shall I trap you forever in this pit, trade one Wolf for another? Or perhaps cast you out of this world entirely?" He chuckled. "Such things have happened before, have they not? You were missing for centuries after the Great Breach."

"Yeah, but does your face hurt?" said Akaz.

"What?" asked Apraxos.

"'Cause it's killin' me."

Aleck laughed out loud; he hadn't heard that one since fourth grade. Apraxos dismissed the comment with a gesture. To Zebdod he said, "Get the boy."

Zebdod jumped into Akaz's mouth. The clawed skull-creature floated in the darkness, trailing its silver thread of a leash.

*Zebdod, Zebdod takes you now*
*Come out of the Hellhound's mouth*
*Master wants you to come out*
*Hellhound's King is over now*
*Zebdod, Zebdod takes you now*

Zebdod danced, claws grasping at the air, floating slowly closer. Aleck and Beth tried scrambling away but found no purchase on anything. Aleck groped in his shoulder bag, grabbing the first thing that wasn't his notebook or video camera: his old wooden yo-yo.

"Zebdod," sang Zebdod, approaching with maddening slowness. "Zebdod, Zebdod."

*Great,* thought Aleck, slipping the yo-yo string onto his finger.

"Zebdod takes you now!" It wildly clawed the air in Aleck's direction, nearly within reach.

Aleck flung the yo-yo hard, hitting Zebdod between the eyes. The skull-thing jolted, then floated there with its legs dangling.

"Yeah!" said Aleck.

"Weird Luck!" said Beth.

Zebdod chuckled, legs twitching, then burst into maniacal laughter. "You cannot harm me with your weapons!" Convulsing with hysterics, it kicked its legs in all directions. "Do you not know the Song? I can only be harmed with a bone of Kaios!" Zebdod laughed and laughed.

"No prob," said Beth, snatching the Cook's rattle from Aleck's belt and plunging it into Zebdod's mouth. The Shinbone seemed to freeze in place, like a knife stuck in wood. Beth let go. The Shinbone stayed put. Zebdod squirmed, shrieking, pinned in the air.

Out through Akaz's mouth, they could see Apraxos trembling with rage. "No!" Apraxos shoved his hand deep into Akaz's mouth and grabbed one of Zebdod's flailing legs. Akaz gagged, the convulsion bumping Aleck and Beth into

Zebdod. Apraxos tugged hard on Zebdod's leg, but the Shinbone of Kaios held him fast.

"Bite his arm off!" said Aleck. Akaz gagged again. Aleck realized Akaz was carefully holding his mouth wide, keeping his fangs away, giving Apraxos no hint of an attack with which to work bad luck magic. Apraxos pulled on Zebdod, and the skull-thing began to move. Aleck grabbed the Shinbone by both ends. Apraxos heaved, pulling Zebdod entirely out of Akaz's mouth, dragging Aleck halfway out, into the cold, dry darkness of the Well. Aleck braced his knees in Akaz's throat and he felt Beth grab his feet. Akaz gagged again and angrily bit Aleck around the waist.

"Ow!"

"Release him!" said Apraxos. He tugged frantically. Zebdod's shriek rose in a sudden crescendo. His jawbone snapped off and spun away across the floor. Zebdod and Apraxos tumbled backwards.

"I will kill you, Akaz!" said Apraxos, jumping to his feet with Zebdod still dangling from his fist.

Akaz spat Aleck out onto the floor. "Shut up, Apraxos."

Aleck looked up to see the Cook standing beside Apraxos with his bow drawn. Then there followed a strange moment, in which time seemed to move very slowly. The Cook released his arrow upon Apraxos. The arrow seemed to move toward Apraxos, then fold back upon itself. It returned, traveling alongside the Cook's arm, toward his shoulder. The Cook stumbled backwards, most of the arrow protruding from his back. Red blood seeped around the wound in his striped gray skin.

"Ah!" said the Cook. "Ah!"

Apraxos looked at him and laughed. "You imbecile, I have the Sovereign Shield!"

The Cook reached around and snapped off half the arrow. Lurching forward, he stabbed Apraxos in the chest with it, tore it out, and stabbed him again, leaving it buried in him. Apraxos let out a deafening shriek and flew straight up like a rocket, still carrying Zebdod. His scream echoed in the Well and receded into the sky.

The Cook collapsed on the stone floor. Akaz and Aleck ran over to him.

"That was *awesome*!" said Akaz.

"What happened?" said Beth from inside Akaz. Akaz spat her out. "Cook!" she said, seeing his blood. "Are you okay?"

"We have failed," said the Cook. "Zebdod is free."

"Well, he's hurt, at least," said Akaz. "And we've got his jawbone. That's useful to us, and makes it a lot harder for him to eat kids, at least for now. And Apraxos—man, I bet he's bummed. You hurt him. His pride, for sure."

"Akaz," said the Cook, "with all our talk of the False Sovereign Shield's effects in the luck plane, and its warding function against you, I forgot its most mundane effects." He laughed a little.

"Sorry about that," said Akaz. "I was wondering why you brought a bow."

"I am embarrassed," said the Cook.

Akaz laughed. "Whaddaya gonna do."

"Let's get him back to the pool!" said Beth.

"Okay," said Akaz. "Shall we?" he asked the Cook.

"Yes, please," said the Cook, struggling to sit up.

"I've got you," said Akaz, swallowing him whole.

# First Herald II

Aleck and Beth ran alongside Akaz, up the ridge and down the other side, this terrain now treacherous in the gathering dark.

Aleck panted out words as he ran. "Why! Don't! You! Carry! Us! Too!"

"Man," said Akaz, "I'm exhausted. You have no idea."

They dodged between the trees. "What do you mean?" asked Beth.

"Bending fate? Standing in the middle of a confluence of forces like that, and tapping it the right way? It's like playing pool, but with a hundred bowling balls, in zero gravity, and your goddamn soul at stake."

"Yeah, but we just float in there!" said Beth. "How can we weigh anything to you? I'm tired too, dammit!"

"Not that simple," said Akaz. "Anyway, we have planning to do."

"Now?" asked Aleck.

"Yes, now!" said Akaz. "Your young self is about to arrive!"

"We don't know when," said Aleck.

"Any minute!" said Akaz.

"We don't know for sure." Aleck felt mortified at how desperate he sounded.

A hill rose before them, and the palisade of Corpsewater appeared atop it. Akaz sped up. "Come on!"

Aleck slowed to a jog and then a walk. "We'll meet you there."

"Keep up!" Akaz said over his shoulder. "And put your hoods up!"

"Come on, the Cook's hurt," said Beth.

"We can meet up with them." Aleck bent at a right angle and panted, hands propped on his knees.

"Your teenage self is about to get here." Beth put her hood up.

Aleck breathed deeply a dozen times, as slowly as he could, which wasn't very. He stood up straight and looked around. The forest had grown darker than he realized. He felt suddenly alone. He tried to spot Akaz up ahead, but could not. His nervousness swiftly increased. Where was Beth? A voice near him said something, and he jumped with fear. "Beth!" Again he heard an unknown voice, coming from the dark between the trees. To his surprise, he saw a lone Keeper, lost in the woods almost beside him. "Keeper, look out!" he stage-whispered. "Some evil forest spirit—"

"Aleck, it's me!" Beth lowered her hood. "Didn't you hear a word I said?"

"Beth! You gave me the scare of my life! Where the hell did you—wait."

"The robe."

"Ah," he said. "The robe."

"Sorry."

"Sorry."

"Did you hear what I said?" asked Beth.

"No. Sorry."

"I said come on, the Cook's hurt."

"Now." Akaz appeared behind them. "We drop off the Cook and summon the Cannibal-King."

"There's no time," said Aleck.

"Not a problem," said Akaz. "We summon him into our past."

"How."

"Not that different from summoning him into our present, actually. The interdimensional shift is the hard part; once you get that, you've got some leeway with when you land."

"Which means he's probably here already," said Aleck. "So why bother."

"Yes, of course he's here," said Akaz. "On his way to Melkhaios. But only because we will have done the spell! If we don't, he won't have appeared in the past! Come on, I'm sick of waiting for you."

He scooped Aleck and Beth into his mouth. They traveled in darkness. After a few minutes, Akaz spat them out and stood there panting, tongue lolling out the side of his mouth, flames flickering down it.

They found themselves at the Corpsewater pool, the boulders around it crowded with villagers. "All hail Great Akaz!" said one.

"All hail the Master Summoner!" said another.

"Hail the Summoner's wife," said an old woman. The crowd cheered. Akaz spat the Cook into the pool.

The back door of the Inn flew open. A teenager in jeans and a black t-shirt burst through, blood crusted on his slashed and maimed face. He mumbled something and sprawled into the pool.

"Fuck," said Aleck.

"You got your guidebook?" asked Akaz.

"What?" asked Aleck.

"For the summoning," said Akaz. "You wanna brief him on what he's walking into. Don't tell me you don't have a book ready...?"

"You mean a whole *book*...?" asked Aleck.

Beth looked at him with furrowed brow. "Didn't your older self say something about a guidebook when you were a kid?"

"Yeah," said Aleck, "and from the way he was talking, it was obvious nonsense. As if a guidebook to the city would fundamentally affect the Cannibal-King's character?"

"You've had your life changed by a book plenty of times," said Beth.

"A *travel guide*?"

"Write whatever you want, man," said Akaz, "and we put it in his brain."

"What?" Aleck looked sidelong at Akaz.

"Khosry the Crow implants whatever knowledge you want into the childhood mind of the Cannibal-King. Not just facts, but opinions and beliefs. They might not fully take, but they'll have an impact."

"Fuck," said Aleck and Beth in unison.

"So it truly is possible," said Aleck, "to summon a more benign Cannibal-King. And I've had my whole life to write one book, maybe just a pamphlet, even, and I blew it."

"Fuck that," said Beth. "I mean, it's cool if you don't mind totally coercing an innocent kid. We're talking some serious end-justifies-the-means shit, Aleck."

"How is summoning someone from another world not totally fucking coercive to begin with?" said Akaz. "And yeah, toppling a murderous oppressive regime justifies it!"

"How long do I have?" asked Aleck.

"Till the King gets to Melkhaios, I'd bet," said Akaz. "However long that is."

"How's that work?" asked Beth.

"Dunno," said Akaz. "That's just time loop shit for ya. I can keep his karmic threads from tangling for a while, but it gets harder the closer they get, and once he's in the vicinity of his own summoning, forget about it. My head already hurts dealing with this shit."

"What is that, like a day from now!?" said Aleck. "It can't be done."

"Put your hoods up," said Akaz.

"Huh?" asked Aleck.

"Now!"

Beth put her hood up. Aleck fumbled with his. As he pulled it over his head, the healed face of his younger self broke the surface of the pool. Beth grabbed Young Aleck by the shirt and dragged him onto a boulder.

Aleck watched, stunned, remembering, as Young Aleck's eyes met the flaming eyes of Akaz. His younger self stared in amazement. Akaz headed toward the Inn, nodding for Aleck and Beth to follow.

# Writer's Block in the City of the Watcher

"There's no way." Aleck shook his head, hunched over his blank notebook, elbows on the *God-Dog* bar. "My notebook isn't even dry yet!"

"Settle down, baby." Beth voice seemed to hold an edge of exasperation, though maybe it was just his own. "You're freaking."

*Yeah,* he thought, *impending death will do that to ya.* But he breathed deeply, or tried to. He scrawled indented spirals in the corner of a page, trying to get his ballpoint pen to start.

"The only reason you believe this scheme is even possible," Beth said, "is because you grew up with bullshit imperialist Hollywood narratives of White Man Saves the Day."

But Aleck barely heard her through his panic. "It's dry enough, I guess," he said, his pen creating a cloud of scribble. "I just have no idea what to do. You can't write a book in a day!"

Beth continued, "As if some übermensch can come in from outside a situation, with superior technology or superior virtue or whatever, and rescue the ignorant locals."

"I saw it happen!" said Aleck.

"No you didn't, dude. You saw some Rambo Mad Max psychopath kill a bunch of oppressive bad guys to make room for other oppressive bad guys. He didn't build a damn thing to sustain a better world, just made a vacuum and inverted the caste hierarchy."

"But here's our chance to change that! We can give him exactly the sort of awareness you're talking about. Change his approach."

Beth rolled her eyes. "His 'approach' isn't the problem, Aleck. You can't perform surgery with a bulldozer, is all."

"So what do you think we should do?"

"Idunno, maybe something based on our best judgment after a thorough assessment of the situation, preferably in coalition with the most righteous locals, rather than just following the lead of my fucking family dog? Oh, I'm sorry, let's not sell him short: do I have this right, he's the fucking local God of Death and Chaos? No prob, who better to make our decisions for us."

Aleck chewed the inside of his cheek.

"But why even ask me, Aleck? This is like your life's goal, apparently."

Aleck shook his head. Suddenly, unexpectedly, a little thing broke inside him, and he told her, "I die at the end."

"What," she said.

"In the middle of the battle," said Aleck emotionlessly, "right before the Train Wreck, right before I split through a portal back home, I saw the Reality Patrol shoot my future self." He clumsily tapped his own chest. "My current self, that is. Like, maybe tomorrow."

Beth stared at him, on the brink of rage but holding it in check for just another moment. "And you never told me this *why*?"

Aleck felt her gaze burning on the side of his face but could not turn to meet it. "I have no idea. I've never told anybody, not even Mikey and Doomer."

"Flatter me more," she said, her rage clicking one notch closer to the surface.

"No, baby." He surprised himself a little. Something in him softened, a tension that had always been there, so implacable he had mistaken it for bone. "I was too scared and scarred to even think about it, never mentioned it to them or anyone. By the time I met you I was already like ten years into that habit."

He saw something soften in her, as if in response.

"Then when I fell in love with you," he said, "I was scared you'd ditch me if you knew I had an expiration date. And it's just gotten more buried and contorted since then. It's been on the tip of my tongue a hundred times, and I've always chickened out." He held her hands. "Please forgive me."

"For now. I'm not sure I can even wrap my head around it right now, really. I may freak out about this later."

He sighed, relieved in the wake of his confession. "Just please don't ditch me?"

"I vowed as much, asshole. Years ago. Full paralysis, acid in the face, whatever. Till death. *You're* the one who's gotta not ditch *me* now, though."

"Huh?"

"Don't die. We're keeping the hell away from any Reality Patrol till we get off this world. Did they come because of the Train Wreck?"

"No, I think they... caused it?" The scene flashed through his mind for the millionth time. He could never quite remember the sequence.

She shook her head. "Fucking typical. 'Imposition of order leads to escalation of chaos.'" Beth pinned him with her gaze. "They come because of the summoning of the Cannibal-King?"

His nervousness returned immediately. "They didn't say?" he answered, weakly.

She eyed him. "We gotta know, baby. We gotta keep them away."

"Just before the Train Wreck started, they were reading instruments and talking about all us parallels meeting—you and me, the Waghalters, me as a kid, both Akazes—"

"*Both* Akazes?"

"Jack and Beth Waghalter, *their* Akaz."

"Oh," said Beth, "right. Well, that means we stay away from your kid self, and Akaz, and we don't even summon the Cannibal-King. Period."

"But if we don't, I mean, the whole reason I ever went to Earth-X00017 and met you is because I was trying to find my way back here, to undo the massacres."

"Fuck," she said. "So even summoning a good Cannibal-King jeopardizes our past." She laughed. "Can't say I've got my heart set on the success of your book, then."

Aleck looked down glumly at his blank notebook. "Great," he said. "Great."

"Fuck it, I say just write him a note. 'Dear Mr. Cannibal-King, please keep an eye on your followers, because I saw the future and they turn into a mob of homicidal massacrers, thanks.' That'll be sure to make everything turn out just peachy."

Aleck looked at her, grave. "How come my life is worth more than all those innocents? That's some fucked priorities."

"Touché, but if you seriously wanna die for a cause, you can do better than this bullshit. Flailing around with hella ambiguous outcomes and completely untrustworthy leadership."

"I have to try."

"Look," she said, "I'm fucking exhausted. I know this is important to you, but I'm at a loss. For all you know, you're on exactly the same track of the Old Aleck you met as a kid."

"I'm not. He said so."

"Well, whatever we do, we're steering the hell clear of all those others, running from any Patrol we see, and getting the hell offa this world a.s.a.p."

Aleck stared at his blank notebook, shaking his head.

"You don't have to write a whole guidebook. He doesn't need to know all about the city. He doesn't need to know what inn to stay at or where to get a good cup of dandelion wine or whateverthefuck. He just needs to know the stuff relevant to his, whatever you want to call it, his conquest."

Aleck nodded numbly. "Baby, I'm sorry." He looked up at her with wet, weary eyes.

"What for?"

"All of this," he said, gesturing vaguely. "Not having an actual plan. Almost getting myself killed yesterday. Potentially getting killed tomorrow and knowing all along since the day we met and never warning you. Freaking out about writing this damn dumb book." He sighed. "Sorry for not going to sleep with you right now in the most comfortable bed we can find in this place." He shook his head. "I am so exhausted," he said, breathlessly.

She put her arms around him. "Look, baby. We're out of danger for the first time since we got here. Let's just do whatever it is we're going to do about the massacres, keep away from danger aside from that, and get our asses the hell out of this fucked up little world. I know you feel guilty about whatever you saw here as a kid, and I know whatever we do will play some sort of part in whatever happens—but you have to let go of the guilt. It's driving you crazy. Both of us." She pulled away. "Realistically, at what point since we got here did we have a chance to intentionally manipulate history? We've been running full-tilt almost nonstop. We're flailing. And we're immersed in something way bigger than us. It's absurd to blame yourself. You don't get to dictate the turn of events, not in the best of circumstances and certainly not in this shit. You can only do what you do."

He nodded glumly. "When I was a kid and I met my future self, he said they had been meticulously adjusting things. Being really careful and deliberate."

"Yeah, that's not us, then," she said, laughing. "Maybe they actually did get here a year before the summoning."

"You're right!" Aleck's eyes lit up. "I'm not him! This isn't the same Melkhaios! I can't stop the massacres I saw as a kid—they happened on another world! A parallel Melkhaios!"

"It's not a circle." Beth smiled. "The multiverse is an infinite number of intersecting, branching spirals. You don't have to worry about jeopardizing our past together, either. It already always was."

"I don't have to write a guidebook at all."

"We don't have to summon anyone."

"The Young Aleck who's here isn't me. He's not my past self."

"He's parallel. You don't have to worry about recreating your past for him, in order to preserve your life history. It's not your past."

"I hope we're right."

"Let's go to sleep."

"I'm gonna leave Akaz a note." In his notebook, Aleck wrote

*Dear Akaz,*

*We're upstairs sleeping. I'm sure you can smell which room we're in. Come wake us when you get in, if you want, but we're not summoning anyone—the deal's off.*

*A&B*

He left his notebook open on the bar. Beth took him by the hand and led him upstairs.

# Skull of Kaios II

They awoke to the sound of their door smashing open. "Come on!" said Akaz, his voice a roar.

Wrenched out of deep, dream-filled sleep, they perceived him as nightmarish: huge, soot-black, eyes and mouth aglow, reeking of burnt flesh. Aleck closed his eyes and opened them again.

"Now!" said Akaz. "Young Aleck is a wreck, Blood Eagle is dying, and Apraxos is on the move!"

"Didn't you see our note?" asked Aleck.

"Get up!" Akaz stepped forward and grabbed the corner of their bed in his brutish jaws. With a twist of his neck he tore away both bedpost and bedclothes, dislodging the mattress and spilling Aleck and Beth painfully across the floor.

Beth jumped to her feet. "Down!" She whacked Akaz across the snout with a pillow. Akaz glowered at her. His legs shook, but he remained standing.

"Apraxos is coming for you," said Akaz. "Now."

"With a couple extra holes in him," said Aleck. "Thanks to the Cook."

"He's healed," said Akaz. "He attacked the Nymph, and healed himself with her suffering."

A chill ran down Aleck's spine. He remembered, as a boy, first setting eyes on her, her tears commingled with baywater—

"The Herax are after us," said Akaz. "All of us. They're probably hunting down anyone in town who *could* be you, Aleck—young or old. To prevent the summoning of the Cannibal-King."

"But we're not going to do it!" said Aleck.

"What?" said Akaz.

"Didn't you see our note?" asked Beth. "We're done with this scheme. Finished. Not gonna summon your damn Cannibal-King."

"Are you walking and talking in your sleep?" said Akaz. "What note? What are you blathering about?"

"On the bar!" said Aleck.

"All I saw on the bar was your guidebook!" said Akaz.

"What?" asked Aleck.

"Come on!" said Akaz. "Blood Eagle and Young Aleck are sitting ducks out there, and Apraxos is going to track us here any minute!" He backed out of the doorway and galloped loudly down the wooden stairs.

Aleck and Beth looked at each other, threw on their jeans and robes, and ran downstairs, Aleck dragging his shoulder bag.

On the bar rested Aleck's notebook. Underneath it sat an inch-thick stack of paper clamped at one corner with a binder clip. Aleck grabbed the manuscript. The title page read:

### *City of the Watcher*
### by Aleck Woad

"What the—?" Apprehensively Aleck flipped through it: page after typescript page of description of the city and its sociopolitical landscape, with footnotes about military strategy and tactics, and warnings peppered extensively throughout about the risk of massacre.

"Come on!" came Akaz's snarling voice from outside.

Rafts lay scattered around the clearing. Upon one of them sprawled Blood Eagle, his flesh shredded, and a small, shivering Keeper.

"That's me," whispered Aleck.

"What, that Keeper?" said Beth. "But he's nobody in particu— oh. The robe."

"I—" Aleck stood on the doorstep, shaking the manuscript, his *Guidebook*. "I—how... where did this...."

"Maybe yet another Aleck," said Beth, with dry sarcasm. "Come back to help you out."

"That has to be it, though." Aleck paged through the manuscript.

"You're not seriously changing your mind? You can't use that, what if Clark planted it here? Or the Reality Patrol!"

"But Beth, this is a different timeline than the one I saw as a kid—"

"So? How the hell does that protect us from Clark's schemes?"

"Get over here!" Akaz stood beside the raft with the wounded. Aleck and Beth wandered over. "Get the thing from him." He indicated Young Aleck.

"What thing?" asked Aleck.

"The Circomangkus," said Akaz.

"Who the f—?" groaned Young Aleck, straining to look up. He pulled his hood back out of his eyes, revealing his freshly-scarred face and shaggy hair. He'd gone gray since they last saw him. "Who the hell are they?"

"Allies," said Beth.

"Come on, I need you to fly these rafts into the kitchen," said Akaz. "I'm sure you can fit them in at an angle."

"No," said Young Aleck, nearly whining. "I'm so sick, I'll puke...."

"Come on. We'll drop you right into the pool." Akaz turned to Aleck. "Get the thing, would you? He's got it around his neck."

"I'd better do it," said Beth. "You probably shouldn't touch him," she said to Aleck.

"Yeah," said Aleck and Akaz together.

Young Aleck tucked his head, enabling Beth to remove the golden amulet from around his neck. "This?" she asked.

"Yeah," said Akaz.

"Who are you guys?" Young Aleck shivered.

Aleck took the Circomangkus from Beth. "I'll fly the rafts. I remember how."

"Pull your hoods back," said Young Aleck.

"Quiet, kid," said Akaz. "Just rest."

Young Aleck struggled up onto his elbows. "You're me," he said to Aleck. "I can tell. That robe can't hide it."

"I'll fly you over to the kitchen, man," said Aleck.

"We have the Skull," said Young Aleck.

"I know," said Aleck. "But we're, uh, not sure if we're going to summon the Cannibal-King."

"What!?" said Young Aleck.

"Ignore him, kid. He's just fuckin' with you." Akaz glared at Aleck, and spat out the halves of the Skull. He hawked deep in his throat and spat out the Jawbone of Zebdod. Aleck stared down at them. "Come on," said Akaz. "We have shit to do."

Aleck just stared at him.

"What?" asked Akaz.

"It's still broken," said Aleck.

"Maybe we shoulda got the Herax to fix it for you?" said Young Aleck, anger flashing out through his exhaustion.

"Come on, baby. Pick up the Skull." Beth whispered to Aleck. "Make like you're going to do the summoning, at least! For the kid's sake. Look at him."

"You my wife?" Young Aleck asked her.

"I'm *his* wife, honey," she said, pointing her thumb at Aleck. "You can call me Beth."

"Grab the Skull and get everyone into the kitchen," said Akaz.

Aleck knelt and put the Skull-halves and Jawbone into his shoulder bag. Gripping the Circomangkus in both hands, he hoisted Young Aleck and Blood Eagle's raft into the air. The raft floated across the clearing toward the *God-Dog*.

"I don't wanna go through that fucking gate again," said Young Aleck.

Aleck moved the raft up to the foot of the kitchen door. "Now what?" he asked Akaz.

"Dump 'em," said Akaz.

"I'm going, I'm going," said Young Aleck, crawling into the kitchen.

"What about Blood Eagle?" asked Aleck.

"Dump him," Akaz growled in annoyance. "He's going right into the pool anyway, dammit." He leapt up onto the raft, grabbed Blood Eagle's leg in his jaws, and dragged his limp, wrecked form onto the kitchen floor with a thump. "Now fly the raft in."

Aleck tilted the raft sideways and slipped it in through the doorway at an angle, walking closely behind it, ducking from side to side to keep an eye on anything it might bump into. Even at an angle it barely fit into the kitchen, and despite his efforts Aleck knocked over a shelf of pots with it.

"Okay, now Beth," said Akaz, "Come on in and close the door behind you. And then open it again, but push on the left side, where the hinges should be."

Beth scowled at him, but did as Akaz described. The door opened to reveal the dark Corpsewater glade behind the *Sign of Death's Door*. Akaz bit deep into Blood Eagle's leg and flung him into the pool. Aleck flew the raft out through the door and leveled it near the ground. Young Aleck crawled onto the raft, rode on it over to the pool, and dropped himself over the side.

They gathered the rafts one by one, upright, into a circle around the pool. Once they had finished, they left them there, and Akaz led Aleck and Beth back out behind the *God-Dog*.

"Okay, now give the Circomangkus to the Cook and let's get out of here," said Akaz.

"The Cook?" asked Aleck. A large crow swept down out of the air, grabbed the Circomangkus from Aleck, and flew in through the kitchen door. The door slammed shut behind it.

"Okay," said Akaz. "Let's go summon the Cannibal-King."

"Akaz," said Beth, "we're not fucking doing it."

"Why do you keep saying that?" asked Akaz.

"Beth," said Aleck, "someone, probably my future self, saw fit to write that guidebook and bring it back for us. Come on."

"Don't be a sucker." Beth looked at Akaz. "We're not going to do it."

"Of course we are," said Akaz. "What are you gonna do instead, go convince the Witch-Queen of Gomothrax to fly across the bay and join us? 'Cause she the only other person I can think of who'd make a difference in this fight. Let me save you a trip: no, she's not going to fly over here and join us. F'cryin' out loud, why the hell else did you come back here in the first place except to summon the Cannibal-King?"

"I came to stop the massacres," said Aleck. He held out the guidebook vaguely in Beth's direction. "Which this could do, maybe."

"How so?" asked Beth.

"Seems like it's got some good ideas in it?"

"So what do you want to do, then," Akaz asked Beth, "just go home?"

"That would work," said Beth.

"And how were you planning to get there?" asked Akaz.

Beth glowered at him, then at Aleck, then back at Akaz.

"I've got a deal for you," said Akaz. "I can get you back home, through a gate under our local Archive. I'll take you there now. On the way there, though, I'm going to try to convince you to help me summon the Cannibal-King. To do the summoning, we need the Engines of Kaios, which are also in the basement of the Archive. So we'll be in the right place either way. Deal?"

Beth took the manuscript from Aleck's hand. She perused it for a minute, ignoring Aleck and Akaz as they watched. Without looking up, she said, "This is your writing style." She handed it back. Sighed. "Your future self probably had some hindsight."

Aleck tapped the manuscript against his leg, staring out across the *God-Dog*'s back yard.

"We'll decide when we get there," Beth said to Akaz. Then, to Aleck: "If we do, we get the hell off this world right after."

Aleck looked into her eyes, nodding. "Yeah." He took her hand. "That's perfect."

Akaz grinned, flames wisping up between his teeth.

# The Cannibal-King

"So I guess we need a boat," said Aleck.

"What?" said Akaz.

"Or a barge or something," said Aleck. "Something with room for us to hide."

"What for?" asked Akaz.

"How the hell are we supposed to get to the Archive?" asked Aleck. "I'm not exactly eager to walk that route again."

Akaz laughed. "You think Corpsewater is the only place I have a gate to?"

Aleck frowned deeply. "You have a gate to the Archive," he said.

"Of course."

"So why the hell did we have to walk all that way? Chased and stabbed and almost killed!"

Akaz narrowed his eyes. "Because you weren't coming here. Were you."

Aleck stared back at him.

"You were going to see the Nymph," said Akaz. "Presumably so she'd help you *not* summon the Cannibal-King, am I right?"

"Oh," said Aleck. "Sorry. Guess so."

"You think *you've* had a hard time? Do you have any idea what this is like for *me*? I'm the goddamned *God of Death*!" Akaz roared. "I should be able to just snap my fingers and the whole Herax army drops dead—but I don't even have fucking thumbs!" He doubled in size, his voice doubling in volume. "*I'm firstborn of the Sun and Earth Dragons!*" He doubled in size again, filling the kitchen. "I'm the oldest, wisest, most powerful being in this motherfucking world!" His voice thundered in the small room. Jars and dishes fell to the floor and shattered. Aleck and Beth covered their ears. He shrank again to the size of a large dog. "But no. Thanks to my curse, what am I? A goddamned talking dog."

"'Wisest'?" Beth gave a snide smile.

Akaz glowered at her, eyes burning hotly.

"Sit." Beth gave him a dirty look. Akaz's hindlegs trembled. After a moment, he sat.

• •

They entered a large, windowless attic room in the heights of the *Sign of the God-Dog*. The flickering firelight cast by Akaz's eyes illuminated a dozen or so black-curtained archways around the perimeter of the room.

Beth gestured. "Isn't this wall shared with the hallway we just walked down?"

"Yeah?" said Aleck uncertainly.

"These doorways weren't in the hall, though," she said, then paused a moment. "Okay, never mind, I get it."

"Lemme see if I can remember which one we want." Akaz sniffed his way around the edge of the room. Periodically he would stop at a doorway and sniff it thoroughly, muttering to himself.

"How come all your gates are up here," asked Beth, "except for the one to the *Sign of Death's Door*?"

"Huh?" Akaz looked up irritably.

"How come," Beth repeated, "all your gates are up here, except for the one to *Death's Door*?"

"Who says this is all?" said Akaz.

"Oh," said Beth.

"Can I work, please?" asked Akaz.

"You don't have to be such a dick all the time," said Beth.

Akaz glowered at her, seemingly about to reply, then turned away and resumed sniffing. "Here," he said, "this way." He nosed his way between black curtains. "Hey!" came his voice from the other side.

Aleck and Beth raced through after him.

A robed figure in a stone hallway stood there shrieking. Glowing stones set into the walls revealed the face of Arch-Dean Werumel. "Guards!" he screamed. "Guards! Guards!" Shallow Ones with long knives burst out through doors down the hallway in both directions.

Akaz looked back and forth, sniffed the air down the tunnel in both directions, turned away from Werumel and said, "Sad to say, it's this way. That jackass dies another day." He frowned at the Shallow Ones before him and growled deeply in his throat. Most of them backed tightly against the walls, trembling; some ran. One, however, stepped in front of Akaz.

"Move," said Akaz. A spasm ran through the Shallow-guard's body, and he staggered to one side. Then, resisting, he leaned toward Akaz with a grimace, swinging. Akaz didn't move. The Shallow's knife-arm jerked wildly and he slashed himself deeply across both knees, just under the kneecap. He collapsed face-first, shouting in pain and dismay. "Better luck next time," said Akaz, walking over him. Aleck and Beth followed Akaz down the hall.

"Kill them!" said Werumel. The frightened guards cowered by the walls, but those behind them raced up to attack.

"Damn it." Akaz dove down the hall and around a corner.

"What the—!" Beth ran after. "What the hell are you doing?"

"Help us!" said Aleck, falling behind.

"Come on, baby." Beth grabbed his sleeve.

Akaz led them down a flight of steps, the Shallow Ones drawing nearer.

"Scare them off!" said Aleck.

"Harder than it looks," Akaz said. "Just run!" He raced around a corner and nearly knocked over the Elder Keeper. Akaz skidded past him and turned around. Beth and Aleck ran around behind Akaz.

The Elder faced the Shallow Ones. "Stop!" he commanded. The Shallow Ones slowed and surrounded him. Werumel strode up, drew his knife, and swung it across the Elder's throat.

"No!" said Aleck.

The Elder fell, gurgling blood.

"Die!" said Akaz. The Shallow Ones staggered away from him. One by one they fell: some wailed and wept as they slashed open their own arteries; others clutched their chests and gasped in agony; a few pairs stood stabbing each other in the chest again and again.

Soon they all lay dead but Arch-Dean Werumel, who stood there shivering in his robe. He threw his knife to the floor. "Spare me, Akaz... *Great* Akaz...." His voice came as a thin whine.

Akaz grabbed the Arch-Dean's head in his jaws and shook him so hard that his body tore away and sprawled several yards down the hall, spraying blood. Akaz swallowed Werumel's head and breathed a cloud of fire down the hallway. Aleck and Beth fell back against the walls, Aleck sliding to the floor. The bodies of the Shallow Ones burned with a horrific, fishy stench. Akaz inhaled their souls and turned away, his eyes burning hot as furnaces. Aleck and Beth backed away from him.

"That way," boomed Akaz's voice as he nudged his ashy snout in the direction they were already moving. "The Engines of Kaios are down there."

••

Aleck and Beth followed Akaz into side-halls, down stairs, and through doors until they found themselves in a large chamber. A tall statue loomed over what looked like an empty pool; the robed, hooded stone figure had a head like a stork. "Greetings, Great Thoth." Akaz bowed his head for a moment at the edge of the pool, then walked around behind the statue and through a doorway. Aleck and Beth followed him into a small room, cluttered with unidentifiable gadgets and artifacts of every size and description. In the middle of it sat a tattered red leather armchair.

"It's like your smoking room," Beth said to Aleck.

"Where the hell are we?" asked Aleck. "Are we still in Melkhaios?"

"Pretty much," said Akaz. "You've never been to these rooms before?"

"I think I'd remember this!" said Aleck.

"I would have thought you would have met him," said Akaz.

"Met who?" said Aleck.

"Thoth," said Akaz. "The Archivist."

"That's a statue of him?" Aleck pointed back to the main chamber.

"No, that's him," said Akaz. "He got turned to stone in the Great Breach."

"Wha...." Aleck wandered back out into the other room.

"Get back here!" said Akaz. "Give me that Skull!" Then he turned to Beth. "Help me look for something." He scanned the shelves.

"So we're doing the summoning?" she asked Aleck.

Aleck looked at her and shrugged. He asked Akaz, "You can send us home right after the summoning?"

"Sure, sure," said Akaz.

"Where's the portal?" asked Beth, warily.

"Huh?" Akaz snapped out of his search.

"The portal to Earth," said Aleck. "Where's our way home?"

"Near," said Akaz.

"Show us," said Beth.

"In a minute," said Akaz. "Look," pointing with his snout to a shelf beside Beth, "there it is, that thing that looks like a wind-up carousel."

"This?" Beth indicated a machine resembling an old electric fan with a dozen blades, each sprouting beaded prongs.

"No, on the shelf above it."

Beth looked and saw a drum-shaped device that looked slightly more like a carousel. She squeezed between the shelf and a large metal machine, and got the drum-carousel down with some difficulty.

"There's a spherical jewel stuck in the center of it, see?" said Akaz.

Beth crouched over it and peered in. "I see it. I have no idea how to get it out of there without breaking this thing, though."

"I don't care," said Akaz. "Just get the stone out of it."

"Hey, don't break it!" Aleck crouched beside Beth. "What is it?" he asked Akaz.

"I don't know," said Akaz. "Just a piece of junk."

"Don't break it," Aleck said to Beth, peering into the gizmo.

"Fucking break it!" Akaz said. "We don't need the machine, just the stone!"

"Aw, man," said Aleck. "So what's that stone?"

"The Third Eye of Kaios. I hid it in that thing hundreds of years ago, to keep it away from Apraxos."

"Whoa," said Aleck.

"So," asked Beth, "now twe're summoning the Cannibal-King?"

"Either that," said Akaz, "or you get me the Witch-Queen. But this is gonna be a shitload simpler."

Aleck stared at the Third Eye. He felt Beth looking at him. He exchanged glances with her. "Shouldn't we?"

"We take the gate back to Earth as soon as we do it," she said.

"Yeah," said Aleck, "absolutely."

Beth shook her head, reached down and pried apart the skinny metal spars holding the Third Eye in place. "Now what?" she asked.

"Put it in the Skull," said Akaz. "And you two need to hold it shut while I weld it back together with my breath."

"How the hell are we supposed to be able to do that?" asked Beth.

"Pray to me," said Akaz.

"What?" said both Aleck and Beth.

"Pray to me, and you'll be immune to fire."

"Christ," said Aleck.

"No, 'Akaz,'" said Akaz. "'Christ' ain't gonna do shit. Get the Skull out!"

Aleck got the Skull halves out of his bag and fumbled them together with Beth, the Third Eye of Kaios rattling around inside. They situated the assemblage atop the carousel-looking thing and held the pieces in place by pushing on them with their fingertips from opposite sides.

"Okay," said Beth. "I don't like this."

"Just say, *Akaz, Akaz, Akaz*," said Akaz, "*Akaz protect us from fire.*"

"Oh, boy," said Aleck.

"Say it."

"Why the hell do we have to say it?" asked Beth. "You're right here!"

"You need to focus your mind properly for it to work! Come on, say it!"

*"Akaz, Akaz, Akaz,"* said Aleck and Beth. *"Akaz please protect us from fire."*

"Don't say 'please,'" said Akaz. "Save that sort of thing for the Sun and Earth Dragons, damn it, or your simpering Earth-Christ. I can't stand the sound of it."

Aleck and Beth stared into each other's eyes, sharing wordless agreement that they too were rather exasperated themselves. They took a deep breath together. *"Akaz, Akaz, Akaz; Akaz protect us from fire. Akaz, Akaz, Akaz; Akaz protect us from fire."*

Akaz spat a jet of white-hot fire onto the Skull and their hands, melting the carousel to slag. The Skull glowed white. Akaz coughed and spluttered.

*"Akaz, Akaz, Akaz,"* said Aleck, pulling the Skull away from the smoldering metal of the wrecked machine. He set it on the floor. The two halves were welded together slightly askew.

"Good enough," said Akaz. "Now use it to find him."

"What? How?"

"Stare into the eye sockets, I guess. Look into the Third Eye."

Aleck stared into the Skull. "What am I looking for?"

"The Cannibal-King," said Akaz.

Aleck looked at him. "Stare into the Skull. And try to see the little gem we just sealed up inside it."

"Don't just see it, see into it. *Through* it."

"What do I do?" asked Beth.

"Nothing," said Akaz. "He's the Master Summoner, not you."

"And try to find someone, I have no idea who. Just 'try to find' him."

"You met him when you were a kid, right?"

"But I don't want the psychopath Waghalter from Earth-X-triple-0-23 this time! I'm trying to find a less murdery Waghalter, from some other Earth!"

"Whatever, just do the thing!" said Akaz. "We don't have much time! Have you entertained the thought—maybe during your little nap at the *God-Dog*, while I was fighting Herax from inside Blood Eagle's body and getting cut to ribbons—did you ever consider what would happen if the Cannibal-King got to Melkhaios before you summoned him? He's almost here! I can feel it!" He closed his eyes. "They're fighting in Bitchwood. Wilders and Givers, and the Merrows of the river, they're fighting the Herax army back to Melkhaios." He opened his eyes. "So hurry up!"

"What happens if he gets here before we summon him?" asked Beth. "So what? You said we could just summon him into our past."

"Not once he gets here!" said Akaz. "If he gets here first, then you *can't* have summoned him, and he never will have been here!"

"What?" said Beth.

"I think I get it," said Aleck, unconvincingly.

"No you don't," said Beth.

"How do you know?" asked Aleck.

"Because it doesn't make any sense," said Beth.

"Just find him!" said Akaz.

"Okay, okay." Aleck stared into the Skull. *Dear god,* he prayed. *Please help me find Jack Waghalter. But not a psycho Jack Waghalter. I mean, not necessarily a full-on pacifist—he's got to get rid of the Herax and all—but one who can instill a sense of respect for other living beings into the Wilders and Givers. And Digglies and Deep Ones. And Deepest, even, I guess.* He sighed.

"See anything?" asked Akaz.

"Shh!" said Beth.

*Please show me a Jack Waghalter,* prayed Aleck, *who has the power of leadership enough to unite the Givers and Wilders, a brilliant strategist who can lead them to victory against the Herax, a fearless leader, et cetera, et cetera. Plus don't forget the pacifist part. Semi-pacifist. Please show him to me.*

Aleck saw flashes in the crystal, and in his mind's eye he thought he saw facets of a young man's life: practicing in some sort of martial arts school; playing war games on a rickety table scattered with miniature metal soldiers and potato chip crumbs; reading books of philosophy; smoking joints; having sex; speaking into a microphone in a D.J. booth.

*Is this him?* "Found him, I think."

"Okay, okay," said Akaz. "Hold your mind on him. Beth, get the Jawbone of Zebdod."

Beth grumbled as she leaned over Aleck's shoulder bag and rummaged through it. Aleck struggled to maintain his concentration.

"Snap that Jawbone on there if you can." Akaz roamed around the small room, sniffing the shelves. "There's a thing here somewhere, we need it so we can talk to him."

Beth found the Jawbone, managed to extract it from the bag, and tried to orient it on the Skull without distracting Aleck. She got it situated, tried to push it into place; it slipped, jabbing Aleck in the hand.

"Ow!" said Aleck. *God please help me hold my concentration on this guy....*

Aleck saw a twenty-year-old Jack Waghalter trapped under ice, kicking himself free. He saw him hold a gun to a man's head and then pull it away. He saw Jack as a young teenager, sitting beside an old man's death bed. He saw him in at least his twenties, sitting on a desk, on what looked like the set of a TV talk show, wearing a wolf mask. He recognized him despite the mask: his tattoos, his voice, his nearly regal bearing.

Beth snapped the Jawbone into place.

Akaz called from the corner of the room. "There he is! Okay, Beth, come here."

"'Do nothing,'" she said. "'He's the Master Summoner, not you.'"

"Come get this thing down." Akaz pointed up with his snout. "See that Victrola with the crow skeleton on it?"

Beth went over and looked up. She saw an intricate metal box, with little gears and camshafts visible inside it. Atop it curved a large metal horn-bell, much like on a Victrola. Something resembling the brass armature of a large, mechanical bird skeleton stood attached to the top of the box, its black-feathered wings spread out like a TV antenna. Beth worked her way to it through the clutter and lifted it down awkwardly.

"Don't drop it!" said Akaz.

Beth scowled at him, carrying the unwieldy box over near Aleck and setting it down.

"Wait a second," said Aleck, backing away from it. "This isn't the Corvus Drive, is it?"

"What? Fuck no," said Akaz. "The fuck I want the Corvus Drive for? I'm trying to defeat an army of a few thousand soldiers, not shatter the entire goddamn planet into a few thousand pieces."

Aleck still felt spooked. "Sure looks like something that could be called a Corvus Drive."

"Don't be a baby. This is Khosry. He's our way of speaking with the Cannibal-King."

"'He'?" said Beth.

"The crow. That's the innards of one of the Crow Terminals. It's still inhabited by its aetheric spirit, Khosry. Khosry has extended his power by integrating with this pandimensional telepaphone. If you can bring him in contact with the Cannibal-King via the Skull, he'll be able to send him dreams."

"'Dreams'?" asked Aleck. "'He'll be able to'? What about us? Aren't we supposed to communicate with him?"

"Sure, sure. Through Khosry. You tell Khosry what you want him to tell the Cannibal-King, and he'll get the information to him."

"What do you mean, 'get the information to him'?"

"Khosry is very wise. He'll be able to initiate the Cannibal-King into the proper epiphanies, at the proper times during his lifetime, to train him to be the sort of general we need him to be."

"I thought I was gonna talk to him!"

Akaz seemed to be losing his patience. "Yes, through Khosry. You tell Khosry what you want him to tell the Cannibal-King, he'll pass it on."

"What, verbatim?" Aleck was losing his patience as well. "How am I supposed to anticipate everything I'd ever want to say to him?"

"Khosry will handle it. Look, you're the Master Summoner, not the Hierophant. Khosry is the Hierophant."

"He's a box!" said Aleck.

"With a bird on it," said Beth.

"And no, it's not verbatim," said Akaz. "He can only speak in questions."

"What?"

"And send dreams, like I said. It's a limitation of the device. We can receive anything, but we can only really transmit questions. And dreams."

"This is totally hare-brained," said Beth.

"You have an alternative suggestion?" said Akaz.

"Yeah," said Beth, "how about not trying to brainwash an innocent kid with a magical bird-on-a-box?"

"Look." Aleck gestured helplessly. "How the hell am I supposed to put my trust for this whole thing into a bird-haunted gear-box? I'm supposed to come all this way, go through all this, invest so much effort into making sure we summon a Cannibal-King who isn't the marauding psychopath I saw when I was a kid, just to delegate—"

"What effort?" Akaz scoffed. "The only goddamn effort you've put in has been *worrying* hard!"

"I almost got killed!"

"You destroyed my fucking Spiral Ride!"

Aleck stared at him, then looked away. "Okay, okay," he said. "What do I do."

"You have to get Khosry in touch with that dude," said Akaz. "I'm sure Khosry will make him into a master of moral restraint."

"Damn it!" Aleck looked back into the Skull. "I lost him!"

"Find him," said Akaz.

"This is the most half-assed shit I've ever seen," said Beth.

Aleck reiterated his prayer, and saw Jack Waghalter again in his mind's eye. He placed the Skull atop the Khosry-box, and felt Khosry enter his mind as well. The bony brass wings folded themselves around the Skull. Aleck repeated the key points of his prayer to Khosry, elucidating his priorities for Jack's Cannibal-King training.

"Understood. Understood. Understood." Khosry flapped his wings with a clatter. "I can see this boy. I will usher him toward illumination." The wing-bones wrapped around the Skull again.

"Move over," said Akaz. "Let me talk to him."

"I don't trust you," said Aleck.

"Tough. Move over." Reluctantly, Aleck did so. Akaz looked into the Skull's eye sockets, then pressed his forehead to the Skull's forehead for a long moment. "Okay. Now the guidebook."

Aleck fished the manuscript out of his bag. "What do we do with it?"

"Clamp it in the Skull's teeth for now, that's probably best."

"What?" asked Aleck.

"Do it!"

"Might as well," said Beth. "Makes about as much sense as any of the rest of it."

Aleck pried open the Skull's jaws and slipped the manuscript between them.

"Okay," said Akaz. "Now we go out by Thoth to do the actual summoning."

"How the hell is this going to communicate information in the guidebook to Waghalter?" asked Aleck.

"Who?" asked Akaz.

"Waghalter!" said Aleck. "The Cannibal-King!"

"Khosry will take care of it," said Akaz. "We just need to get the summoning done, then you can go home."

• •

Aleck and Beth sat facing each other in the dry pool, knees almost touching, Akaz squatting beside them at Thoth's feet. Khosry sat in the middle.

"Okay, now part two of two," said Akaz. "You found him, now we bring him over. Hold hands, shut your eyes."

Aleck and Beth reached over Khosry, took each other's hands, and dropped their clasped hands to their knees. They looked each other in the eyes for a long moment, then closed them.

*"As Three-Eyed Lady Oshta is Queen of Love and Magic,"* said Akaz, *"your love for each other makes this magic possible."*

"That sounds awfully sentimental, coming from you," said Beth. Aleck could hear her wry smile.

"Whatever. I'm just reciting. Nothing but nuts and bolts as far as I'm concerned."

Aleck sensed Beth's silent sigh through her fingertips.

"Here's the basic cosmology," said Akaz, "so you can picture it. Thoth holds the Key to the Astral Plane. Astral Plane touches all possible worlds. You guys pray to Thoth, he lets us in, we do our thing, your guy comes through. More or less."

"How do we pray to him?" asked Aleck.

"Repeat after me."

"If 'our love makes this possible,'" said Beth, "then it sounds like I *am* necessary, Mr. Don't-Do-Anything-He's-the-Master-Summoner-Not-You."

"Okay, okay. Whatever. Shut your eyes."

Aleck opened his eyes to see Beth giving a Look to Akaz. "'I'm sorry' would suffice," she said.

"Whatever. Shut your eyes. Repeat after me."

Akaz recited, and Aleck and Beth repeated, stumblingly at first:

*In the name of Nyarlathotep, Great Akaz, Herald of the Gods;*
*In the name of his manifestation, the Cannibal-King;*
*We beseech thee, Great Thoth,*
*King of Magic,*
*Author of the Mother of All Books.*

*In the name of Azathoth, the Sun Dragon;*
*In the name of his manifestation, Kaios the Summoner;*
*We beseech thee, Great Thoth,*

*All-Knower,*
*Bearer of the Eleven Keys to the Archive.*

*In the name of Shub-Niggurath, the Earth Dragon;*
*In the name of her manifestation, Oshta the Moon;*
*We beseech thee, Great Thoth,*
*Teacher of the Gods,*
*Walker-Between-Worlds.*

*In the name of Yog-Sothoth, Lord of the Astral World;*
*In thy name, Thoth the Archivist, his manifestation;*
*We beseech thee, Great Thoth,*
*Opener of the Ways,*
*Maker of the Key to the Astral Plane:*

*Open the Way to us.*

A wave of dizziness crashed over Aleck. Everything blurred. A curtain of static flowed down upon him, as though television snow covered his eyes, matched by a buzzing in his other senses. He began to panic. *Beth!* he tried to say.

He sensed her. *I'm here,* he heard, in his head. Her voice. Did he imagine it? He thought he could see a tiny light, like a distant star. What was happening? *Is Thoth driving us insane?* Aleck thought. *Or are we statues like him now?*

*Hey,* came Beth's voice, or the thought of her voice.

He called to her with his mind. *Beth.*

*Don't worry,* she said. *We're together.*

The tiny light erupted into a hot star, like a spherical bonfire beside him. *Holy shit! Are you okay?*

*Sure,* came Beth's voice from her fiery soul. *Nothing happened to me.*

*You just blew up!*

*No,* she said, *you just came over close to me. I stayed the same size. You changed your perspective.*

"Guys." They perceived Akaz floating beside them, shaped not like a star but still a wolf, sitting back on his haunches in the middle of the void. "Now just keep saying, *Thoth, we beseech thee, Thoth, we beseech thee,* etc., etc."

*Thoth, we beseech thee,* said Beth.

*Dude, what's going on?* asked Aleck.

"F'Chrissakes, Aleck," said Akaz, "you're summoning the Cannibal-King!"

*Okay...* said Aleck. *And how do I...?*

"Thoth-we-beseech-thee!" Akaz's snarl sounded flat and distant in the void.

*Thoth,* said Beth, *we beseech thee.*

The robed statue appeared behind Akaz, floating in the strange void.

*Thoth-we-beseech-thee!* said Aleck.

Not words, nor even something as concrete as thought, but rather pure intention emanated from the statue: *I am Thoth, manifestation of Yog-Sothoth.*

"Great Thoth." Akaz turned and bowed his head to the feet of the statue. "Please open for us the walls between the worlds."

The essence of *Why?* came from the statue.

*We come to summon the Cannibal-King,* said Beth.

Elation poured from the statue like hot sunshine. Another light appeared under the Beth-star; and one by one, above them, more appeared in a straight column. Soon there glowed seven lights of different sizes and colors. Around them grew an intricate latticework of fiery arabesques, outlining Beth's aetheric body. Aleck could feel his own layers of being as they glowed, burned, intertwining with Beth's astral form. Jagged stripes of fire coiled around and through them, endlessly flowing and spiraling. Innumerable resonances hummed in the shimmering space.

"Great Thoth, please bring us the Cannibal-King," said Akaz.

*Where?* came from the statue.

"Find him, kid," Akaz said to Aleck.

Aleck was about to ask *How?* when he saw Khosry and the Skull floating in front of him, in between his and Beth's clasped hands. He focused his attention on the Skull, and the entire apparatus floated up toward his eyes of fire. He looked between Khosry's bony brass wings, into the Skull's eye sockets, and into the depths of the Third Eye of Kaios.

Aleck saw a dark spiral spinning. For a moment he felt afraid of it, but he peered closer. Outward from the swirl spread a shinbone, a calf, a hand holding a tattoo gun.... Jack Waghalter, getting a spiral tattooed on his anklebone.

"Is that him?" asked Akaz.

Aleck looked. Through Jack's flesh he could see a golden shinbone. A helix of phantom beads spiraled up its length.

*An echo from the Cook's rattle,* said Beth.

*What?* asked Aleck. *Are Jack and Kaios the same person?*

"Y'all are cognate," said Akaz, looking over his shoulder. "That's him. You've got the right world." He turned back and bowed his head again. "Great Thoth—can you maintain our contact with this world?"

*The Way is open,* came from the statue.

Aleck sensed something akin to *That's not what I asked* drifting off of Akaz in an aetheric grumble. "Okay, Aleck," he said, "bring him over."

*What?* asked Aleck. *How?*

"Dunno," said Akaz. "You're the Master Summoner, you tell me."

*I don't know gate magic!* Aleck said, angrily. *I just have a knack for finding them!*

*Baby,* said Beth, *maybe lighten up on that for a bit. Look around you. We're floating in magic.*

"Well, you're the one destined to get him through," said Akaz. "Since Thoth can't or won't guarantee we'll keep contact with that world, I recommend you start thinking, 'cause I don't know how it's supposed to happen. Though even if I did, telling you could mess it up."

*Tell me anyway!* said Aleck.

"I said I don't know," said Akaz. "And if I did, it might activate the Shield of Apraxos, or might just undermine your Summoner-ness. It's gotta come from you."

*Well at least suggest something!* said Aleck.

Akaz glowered at him. "Khosry, help me out, here. Show Aleck your stuff."

*How can the Cannibal-King come through to our world?* asked Khosry.

*Through here!* said Aleck, gesturing with a sweep of his shimmering arm.

*Through where?* asked Khosry.

Aleck pointed at the Skull. With a glance he saw through it, to Jack teaching a martial arts class; he recognized it immediately as Golden Whirlwind, the syncretic style Beth studied. *Through here! Through the gate!*

*How will you become small enough to fit in there?* asked Khosry.

Akaz snickered.

*Don't tell me I'm constrained by size and scale here,* said Aleck, shoving his arm into an eye socket up to the elbow. *I've been astral before.*

*Showoff,* thought Beth, with a mental laugh.

*What gate?* asked Khosry.

Aleck flailed his hand around inside the Skull. To his surprise he felt his hand contact something, hard. He whipped his arm back out.

Akaz howled with laughter. "I bet that gets talked about more than once."

*I just whacked somebody upside the head, didn't I.*

"Looked like it to me," said Akaz.

*Who?* asked Beth. *Was it Waghalter?*

*Do you think the Reality Patrol would notice something like that?* asked Aleck.

"Not if you're not under surveillance," said Akaz, cocking an eyebrow.

Beth and Aleck looked at each other. *We'd better hurry,* she said.

"It's not a gate," said Akaz. "It's just a resonance. Like a membrane. Less permeable than a full-on gate." With complete disregard for size and scale, he ducked his head into the Skull's left eye socket and pulled it back out again. "I'd be hard pressed to get through, and I'd be worried about getting back."

*But I can touch him,* said Aleck. *I hit him in the middle of a sparring match.*

"Right," said Akaz. "You could probably even squeeze through. But I wouldn't bet on being able to get back, much less bring him with you."

*So I'll reach in, grab him, and pull him through.*

*Wasn't he a Golden Whirlwind master?* asked Beth. *If someone grabbed me from offworld I'd break their wrists.*

Aleck reached with hands of coruscating light into his own glowing skull and grabbed his astral brain in exasperation. *What the hell am I supposed to do?*

*What can you do?* asked Khosry.

*Calm down, for starters,* said Beth.

Aleck shifted into a symmetrical pose and held it. The shimmering of his astral body fell into a harmonious rhythm.

*What can you do?* repeated Khosry. *How can he get through?*

Aleck thought.

*How can he get through?* said Khosry. *What can you do?*

*Wait,* said Beth. *He gets through on his own.*

Aleck's aetheric hands gripped hers. *I can teach him.*

*At your service,* said Khosry, bowing its bird-skull.

*Hey,* said Beth, *I thought you could only speak in questions.*

*To Waghalter, indeed,* said Khosry. *But you and I are in the same world. I was merely practicing.* The metal skeleton hitched its shoulders up and down as though laughing.

*Akaz, give him the guidebook, for starters,* said Aleck.

Akaz nodded. "Okay, good thinking." Akaz snatched the guidebook in his teeth from between the Skull's jaws and then forced his head into its mouth. He pulled it back out immediately, without the manuscript. "What next."

*We need to plant seeds,* said Aleck. *Not much time. We have to put the right ideas in his head.*

"Khosry's specialty."

*Peacefulness,* said Aleck. *Compassion, respect for other living beings, teach him that sort of thing.*

"Hold on," said Akaz. "We'll get to that. But first we need to teach him how to get here."

*We need both,* said Aleck.

A strange buzzing sound proved to be Khosry's voice, speaking startlingly, incomprehensibly fast. Blips in his cadence indicated the end of each interrogative.

"I think he's got it covered," said Akaz.

*Okay,* said Aleck. *So, in addition to teaching him how to be a moral leader and a military leader, spark his interest in the idea of other worlds. Interest him in comic books, fantasy literature, the occult, drugs, comparative religions, theoretical physics, all that stuff.*

Khosry's buzzing voice continued.

*Make sure to teach him how to use drugs responsibly,* said Beth.

Aleck gazed into the Skull. Jack sat on a desk, on what looked like a television talk show set. He wore a cartoonish, plastic wolf snout covering his nose. Men in suits sat in the three guest chairs. Jack held a small lever-action rifle with spiral patterns on the stock.

*Pacifist,* said Aleck. *Make sure he's a pacifist.*

"Not a pacifist," said Akaz.

*You know,* said Aleck, *a self-defense only, protect-the-in-nocents type. Violence only as a last resort.*

"Yet with no fear of the ultimate encounter," said Akaz, sternly.

*What?* asked Aleck. *'The ultimate encounter'?*

*Killing people,* said Beth.

"No hesitation," said Akaz.

*Only when absolutely necessary!* said Aleck.

"And make sure he tries to learn how to open gates," said Akaz.

Khosry buzzed.

Aleck gazed into the Skull. He saw a riot, a horde, circling a huge fire—was it the crowd he'd seen at the Circus as a boy, dancing around the Wargus-Fire? No; no Herax boats circled overhead. Flat desert stretched into the distance. Multicolored electric lights flashed on the bodies of the crowd. He saw Jack dancing around the fire in a circle. Around, around, threading between other dancers and the fire, always closest to the fire.

The riot thinned, the conflagration dimmed to a network of fires crisscrossing a vast, hellish bed of smoking ash. The sky paled from starry black to gray. A jagged line of red appeared on the hilly horizon. A sparse crowd remained, dancing, bantering, huddling into blankets. And still Jack trudged around the fire, slowly now but relentless, around, around.

The phrase "Pacing the Circle" came into Aleck's mind. Where had he heard that?

"This is it!" said Akaz. Aleck looked up. Akaz and Beth were also bent over the Skull, staring into it.

*What?* asked Aleck.

"This is how he does it!" said Akaz, jubilant.

*Does what?* asked Beth.

"He's forging a gate to Kaios! Can't you see?" Akaz laughed.

Aleck and Beth looked at each other and shrugged. *Looks peaceful enough,* said Beth.

Jack, in a suit, stood on the wide steps of an official-looking building, shouting into a megaphone. A crowd filled the street. Next they saw hundreds of rioters, storming down city streets lined with shattered windows. Rows of police cars burned steadily. They saw riot police on fire, trampled; shields and weapons were taken up by rioters against the next row of cops.

*Wait a minute...* said Aleck. *Not sure this is the ideal Cannibal-King....*

Jack sat in a dimly-lit room, tied to a chair, naked. A sweating man wearing a loosened necktie burned the side of Jack's neck with a cigarette. Jack scowled and spoke defiantly. The man poked the cigarette into Jack's eye.

*Yow!* said Aleck.

A white van hurtled across a dry desert flat, chased by black sedans and helicopters. Jack, wearing an eyepatch like a pirate, manned a ring-mounted machine gun in its roof. A helicopter crashed onto a pair of pursuing cars.

*No!* said Aleck. *This looks like Earth-X00023! This is not the guy I want!*

"He's at the gate!" Akaz exulted.

All went white for a moment.

Then a crowd of Givers surrounded the parked van, looking at the horizon. Herax ships flew in low. Jack took aim at one with his lever-action rifle. Flame burst forth from it, and the recoil knocked him off his feet. The mast of the nearest ship snapped, crashed onto the deck; mast, sail, and rigging slid to the ground, dragging the ship with them. Givers charged the fallen ship.

Akaz jumped to his feet. "He's here! Gotta go!" He disappeared.

# The Battle of Melkhaios

What? Aleck had the impulse to stand up and follow, then realized he had no idea how. *Wait!* He desperately looked around the astral plane. *How do we—?*

*Thoth, we beseech thee—* Beth began.

*Thoth-we-beseech-thee-please-return-us-to-the-material-plane!* said Aleck.

The hooded statue nodded.

They found themselves sitting in the dry basin at Thoth's feet, Akaz racing out the door. Between them rested the mechanical Victrola-box—with no sign of skull or crow.

"Wait!" Aleck jumped to his feet. "Where's the damn portal back to Earth!"

Akaz stopped in the doorway, looking back at them. "Sorry, we can do that after the battle. Gotta go." He turned and ran off.

Aleck ran after him. Beth followed, quickly passing Aleck. "Akaz!" she said. Aleck saw Akaz glance back at her and speed up. "Stay!" said Beth. Akaz's limbs froze. He skidded and slammed into a wall. Beth ran up to him, and Aleck soon joined them, panting. Akaz ran off again. They chased after, Beth interrupting him periodically with a variety of commands but never stopping him for long, Akaz quickly shaking it off and bounding out of sight. Aleck managed to keep from falling too far behind Beth, but he was suffering for it. At least he had somehow managed not to develop a stitch in his side, yet. This elastic chase continued, Beth catching sight of Akaz, Akaz freezing and falling over and cussing a blue streak, Aleck catching up with them out of breath, Akaz leaping up and zooming off, again and again, all the way back to the *God-Dog*. When they arrived in the room of curtained portals, Akaz sped downstairs to the ground floor. Aleck and Beth chased after him.

They found him out on the back stoop. The last red of sunset faded on the bayward horizon. Wilders crowded the yard behind the *God-Dog* in humanoid and animal form. Their dancing and play-fighting came to a halt, replaced with a chant: "Akaz, Great Akaz! Akaz, Great Akaz!"

"Great Akaz, the Cannibal-King has come, as foretold by Kaios!" said a nearby Wilder. The chant turned to a mingling of "Akaz!" and "Cannibal-King!" and soon dissolved into general cheering.

"This is all well and good," said Aleck.

"But you gotta show us the way home first," said Beth.

Akaz ignored them. "Where is the King?" he roared to the assembly.

"He chases the Herax!" came the reply. "They retreat into the city!"

"Why are you here, then?" asked Akaz.

"Our King commanded us to guard the *God-Dog*, O Great Akaz!" said a Wilder.

"Most of us have gone to light the Wargus-Fire!" said another.

"Akaz!" said Aleck and Beth together. He showed no notice.

"Some of us are yet arriving from the far parts of the Isle," said a huge gray-furred wolf. "As replacements arrive, those who have waited here move along to our King's side."

"The Ride is broken," said another Wilder. "We freely cross the Mounds."

Akaz nodded, then dashed up the side of the Spiral Mound toward the heart of the city. "Heel!" said Beth. Akaz paused momentarily at the crest, and Aleck and Beth ran to catch up with him, Wilders staring in wonder at these mortals with power over their god. Aleck and Beth climbed up and down the darkening wooded ridges, stumbling over gnarled roots, Akaz repeatedly racing ahead, Beth reining him back with "Heel! Heel!"

"I really would prefer ya went back!" said Akaz. "Or at least let me go on ahead! Haven't I missed enough of this fight for your taste?"

Past the Spiral Mounds they ran into a neighborhood of narrow dirt streets, flanked by vine-tangled stone buildings. They heard occasional screams. Aleck wheezed a bit. As they stomped through mud there came an unmistakable tang on the air: Aleck and Beth looked at one another, together realizing the street was muddy from blood. "Ugh."

Beth put her hood up. Aleck followed her example. Akaz ran ahead. "Heel!" said Beth. Chasing him around a corner, they saw a pack of Givers—hairless, sexless, covered with patterns of branding-scars—dragging bodies in through a building's smashed front door. From inside came horrifying, ravenous sounds.

"No!" Aleck said. The Givers in the street froze in place and looked at them.

"Great Akaz!" said one of them.

"No," said another, "just a Wilder and some Keepers."

"Fool!" said another. "The King commanded us not to feed, and now He has sent His hound to feed upon us in turn!"

"You are the fool. What Cannibal-King would order us not to feed?"

"He did!"

"If so, what of it?" said the bloodiest of the Givers. "He has led us to victory. We have no further need of Him."

"Great Akaz, spare us!"

"I don't care what the hell you eat," said Akaz. "Just tell me where the fuck your King went."

The Givers pointed.

Akaz ran off. Aleck and Beth ran after, shouting at him. They arrived at a fountain with a statue of Goromath in the center, a massive ox of a man in a streamlined uniform, water spilling from both hands. A Wilder in wolf-form floated in the pool, twitching slowly, several Herax javelins sticking through its torso at the same angle. Aleck and Beth both nervously checked the sky.

Past the fountain loomed the wide wall surrounding the New Market. Firelight flashed through an open gateway. Square towers flanked it, crows flocking on the roofs, Givers lurking in the windows and doors. Shouts and screams came from the far side of the wall.

"That doesn't sound good," said Aleck.

"Sorry, baby," said Beth. "But let's go back to the *God-Dog* and wait it out."

Akaz bolted through the gate into the New Market. The Givers guarding it chanted, "Akaz! Akaz!" and loudly clattered their little hand-drums.

"No. C'mon. I have to see this. I have to know if it's any better." Aleck ran after Akaz.

"Aleck!" Beth caught up with him just inside the gate.

A roaring fire swept around a crashed Herax ship, spreading over the booths nearby. Herax soldiers desperately fought to escape while fireproof Givers and Wilders wrestled them back into the flames. Across the New Market, other fires spewed pillars of black smoke into the sky. Sounds of fighting and Giver-drums came from every wreck. Herax ships and one-masted boats flew back and forth overhead, some low, some very distant. Shapeshifting Wilders harried the deck of every ship, switching constantly between bird, wolf, and humanoid-form, with the occasional stag or bear.

The abrupt, unmistakable clamor of machine-gun fire broke through the sea of noise in the New Market. A low-flying Herax boat listed sharply, its severed mast toppling over. The boat crashed through a pair of market-stands and skidded to a stop fifty yards in front of Aleck and Beth, the cobblestones cracking open its hull. Givers and Wilders ran up to it and set it on fire.

Akaz raced by. "Akaz!" said Aleck. Akaz glanced at him and ran off toward the mouth of a dark aisle. Aleck ran after, followed by Beth. Sounds of gruesome feasting came from the shadows.

"I think this is worse than last time." Aleck slowed to a walk, gripping his sides. "I can't run any more."

"Good!" said Beth. "So we amble on back to the *God-Dog*, before you get killed!"

"We have to do something about this." Aleck's voice sounded hollow even to himself.

"Such as?" asked Beth.

Aleck looked at her. "Appeal to the Cannibal-King to stop it."

"And we find him how?" asked Beth.

A block ahead, the white Ford van sped across the aisle, rattling on the cobblestones. Aleck gestured at it. "See?"

Something metal fell off the back of the van with a noisy clatter. Akaz ran down the street after the van. Aleck struggled into a trot. In the intersection he and Beth found two bicycles, a rickety old Schwinn and a pink girl's bicycle with white tires and ratty metallic streamers sprouting from the ends of the handlebars.

"These are the exact bikes I saw us on." Aleck tried to right the bikes, but their pedals had locked into each other's spokes. "I always wondered where we got them."

Beth put a foot on the frame of the top one, pinning them both. "Aleck. Stop."

"Beth, this timeline is different."

"Not different enough! Not if there's so much Meta-Novikov self-consistency between parallel worlds or timelines for the same goddamn pair of bikes to drop at our feet."

Aleck frowned at the bicycles. "I don't know if they're the *exact* same bikes."

"Dude."

"You telling me you can just ignore these massacres? For all we know, they're just getting started. We could really save some people."

Beth looked around uncomfortably. Screams and sounds of carnage echoed around them. "What makes you think Waghalter can even do anything about it?"

"He's their frickin' messiah, Beth. He might have a little bit of pull."

She nodded, glumly. "But who says *we* have any pull with *him*?"

Aleck shrugged. "We summoned him? And before that we brainwashed him?"

She pursed her lips. "Okay, but what's your plan for not getting killed?"

"We know what to look out for," he said, not entirely convincing to either of them.

"Yeah, we need to avoid meeting the Waghalters. So much for that idea."

"Well," said Aleck, "we need to avoid gathering with them *and* their Akaz *and* our Akaz *and* my younger self."

"Unless the Novikov factor makes sure you get killed some other way. Dying is not unheard of, y'know, on a battlefield."

He sighed. "I can't stand by, though."

They looked into each other's eyes awhile.

"Yeah," she said, "me neither, I guess."

Aleck and Beth puzzled the bicycles apart and hopped onto them. Aleck kicked down on the pedal of the Schwinn, and it dropped without resistance; he bashed the inside of his knee against the crossbar. "Ow!"

"Great."

"I'm okay," said Aleck. "What the hell—"

"Your chain's off the gear." Beth dismounted and held the handle of the girl's bike out to him. "Here." He dismounted with a frown. Beth crouched, re-threaded the chain on the gear, hopped onto the Schwinn and rolled away.

"Hey!" said Aleck.

"Come on!" said Beth over her shoulder.

Aleck frowned down at the pink bicycle and got onto it, standing up on its plastic white pedals. He pumped furiously, pain shooting through his side and his knee, bike shuddering over the cobblestones, his shoulder bag swinging around annoyingly. He managed to catch up to Beth, and saw Akaz far ahead. The van turned out of sight.

"Heel!" hollered Beth. Akaz slowed, glowered back at them, then broke back into a run.

"Even you can't keep me away from Wargus-Fire!" Akaz disappeared around the corner after the van.

"Come!" said Beth. "Heel!"

Aleck and Beth turned the corner and found Akaz, angrily trudging forward, one heavy step after another. "Heel!" said Beth again.

Akaz gave her a furious look. "Damn it!"

"Go!" said Beth. "But don't get out of our sight."

Akaz raced forward to the limit of visibility, then skidded out of sight. They turned a corner to see him frozen, straining as if against an invisible leash—shooting down the street as soon as he came into view.

Thusly they rode up to the Senate, Akaz leading by fits and starts. Firelight spilled out of the archways. Everything inside the huge, bleak building seemed to be burning. They dismounted and followed Akaz across the river, walking their bikes on the bridge alongside the Senate building. Heat radiated through the stone wall.

Emerging from the bridge, they jumped back onto their bicycles and followed Akaz as he ran down the street. The white van burst out from the Senate archway behind them, trailing tattered, burning cloth. "Wait—" said Aleck. Beth whistled at Akaz, who ran back to them.

Three-masted Herax warships rounded the Senate on either side. Soldiers chanted from the decks: *"We come as one! We come as one!"*

As the van raced up to them Aleck saw Jack Waghalter manning the machine gun in the van's rooftop ring mount, wearing an eye patch and sleeveless army shirt, a grimace of berserk glee twisting his face. Waghalter swung the gun around and unleashed a quick torrent at one of the ships. His bullets seemed to explode in fireballs wherever they hit, punching holes in the keel, blasting Herax soldiers in half, cracking masts. The top spar fell from the mainmast, trailing burning rigging and mainsail. The ship slowly sank as it proceeded down the street. A volley of javelins flew back toward the van, falling short and clattering to the street, or twisting in place as they neared their target and sailing back into the torsos of whichever Herax had flung them. As Waghalter redirected his aim to the other ship, the burning ship angled away across the city, sails afire, sinking gradually streetward.

Crows swarmed over the falling ship as it descended, scattering while it crashed into the side of a small stone mansion, then returning to fight the survivors. A pair of Herax longboats came in low over the roofs, showering the deck of the ship with javelins. Wilders and Herax alike fell. Half a dozen flying rafts joined the skirmish, Givers crouched upon them with hands afire. The Herax soldiers hurled javelins from their longships; the Givers flung back thick balls of flame.

The van sped away down the street toward the Circus of Burnt Skulls. Akaz ran after it. As Aleck and Beth struggled to keep up they saw Givers and Wilders in the shadows, running in the same direction.

The clatter of an engine approached from behind. Aleck and Beth looked back to see a large motorcycle, ridden by a heavy-set, middle-aged bearded man wearing dark goggles. "Make way for Doomer!" came his bellowing voice. As he rode past Aleck and Beth, he slowed momentarily to grin at them. "Hey Woads, try not to fuck our bikes up," he said brightly. He wore several guns. He sped off before Aleck or Beth could say anything, meeting up with the van at the end of the street.

"Where the fuck did he—"

"Is that even *our* Doomer?" asked Beth.

They looked at each other. "Fuck."

••

Herax soldiers stood in rows in the gates of the Circus and atop its walls. Herax craft, flying in formation, filled the air above the arena. Ships and boats circled in alternating directions, one ring hovering over another: a dozen rings, hundreds and hundreds of Herax, every throat roaring, *We come as one.*

Waghalter's van idled near the main gate. Givers and Wilders massed in the shadows of the plaza surrounding the Circus. Waghalter's voice thundered from a megaphone: "Well, come on, then!"

The Herax fell silent. Aleck listened to the ships creaking in the windy sky. He could hear fires burning back at the New Market. Distant shouting scattered across the city.

Doomer revved his motorcycle.

Akaz turned to Aleck. "Stay out of my way." He looked at Beth. "No more commands." She opened her mouth to protest. "No! Damn it, leave me be! I've been working on this for four hundred fucking years, let me at least enjoy this part of it!"

Beth closed her mouth and furrowed her brow. She turned to Aleck. "Well, what do you wanna do, baby?"

Aleck felt sure that he looked broken.

"Bye," said Akaz, and ran off. They saw him run up to the alley behind a store called *Real Giver Drums* and bark orders at the warriors lurking there. They produced a sudden rattle of Giver drums that just as abruptly stopped. Other drums rattled a block away, then a block further, on into the distance.

Herax ships continued to converge at the Circus, adding another ring to the formation.

"Well," said Aleck, weakly, "at least if the Givers and Wilders are all here, they're not off killing anybody else."

"Let's go home, baby."

Aleck shook his head. "There must be something we can do."

A flying raft alighted behind Waghalter's van. Givers and Wilders scattered from it back across the plaza. Waghalter ducked out of sight. The van backed up onto the raft, and then the raft heaved it up into the air. Waghalter emerged from the van's roof with his hunting rifle. He spat fire onto it, and flames danced up and down the barrel. The flying van began orbiting the Circus, parallel to the lowest ring of the Herax formation. Waghalter levered the action on his rifle and it flashed with fire. He brought it to his shoulder, aimed, and a fiery blast spat from it. The recoil knocked him against the edge of the hole in the van's roof, and Aleck and Beth could faintly hear him shout, "Ow!" The mast of the nearest Herax ship split asunder and fell in flaming pieces to the deck. The ship tipped nose-downward and dove into the stands with a crash of splintering timbers and shouts of crushed Herax.

They saw Akaz race across the plaza toward Doomer on his motorcycle. Doomer said, "What the—?" and aimed a pistol at the monstrous wolf, but too late. Akaz leapt into his mouth. Doomer's body convulsed wildly for a moment, then stopped. He gave his head a vigorous shake. Stiffly he took aim at a Herax longboat. Fire erupted from his pistol. An explosion took a chunk out of the boat's keel, and it dipped in its flight. Slowly it began sinking. "Yeah!" Doomer tossed the pistol to his other hand, revved the motorcycle, and rode off around the Circus, firing left-handed up at the Herax.

The other flying rafts sped around the Herax formations, Givers flinging fire at sails, Wilders laying arrows into soldiers' unarmored faces and throats. From the shadows around the plaza stormed Givers and wolves, sprinting for the front gates. Javelins rained down upon them. Givers and Wilders fell to the cobblestones by the dozen, where they lay squirming, some still crawling for the gates. A wave of crows stormed through the air over the edge of the Circus wall. Herax javelins snatched them out of the air; speared crows fell upon their kin on the ground. Wolves, deer, and Givers raced in through the open gates, their bodies exploding with roaring fire among the ranks of Herax soldiers.

The flying rafts fell back from their assault, landing outside the Circus and tilting upward to dump everyone onto the street. The empty rafts flashed back into the air. Aleck felt a twinge of anxiety. A blur of chaos erupted over the Circus, and then a dozen Herax ships tumbled down, trailing tattered sails. They fell upon other ships, plummeting together within the arena or out onto the cobblestone plaza. Aleck gasped. "The Token! I felt it—"

"Wha—" said Beth.

"The thing that gave me white hair. The Token of Time Dilation—Blood Eagle used it, I could feel it! Attacked the Herax ships with the rafts, just like I did—"

The Herax momentarily stunned, their attackers surged forward: a horde of Givers and Wilders rushed across the plaza, setting fire to fallen ships, slaughtering their crews, and swiftly moving on to the Circus gates. Flying rafts came in low, laden with what looked like freshly-chopped-down trees, and slipped over the rim of the Circus, crows in a cloud around them. A chant arose from the attackers.

"What are they saying?" asked Beth.

"'Wargus-Fire,'" said Aleck.

"What the hell is that?"

"The sacred fire of Akaz."

Light erupted up from the Circus, along with the loud crackle of pine trees bursting into flame. The wild folk cheered cacophonously, resuming their chant of "Wargus-Fire! Wargus-Fire!" with renewed aggression.

Doomer on his motorcycle sped around from the far side of the Circus, roaring in Akaz's voice: "The Fifth Sphere is mine once again! Can you feel it, Goromath?" He laughed thunderously. "MINE! *Prepare for your final defeat!*"

Givers and Wilders continued pouring into the front gates of the Circus. The formations of Herax ships broke apart, some swinging low to shower their enemies with spears, others surrounding Waghalter's flying van. The Herax attempted to ram the van with longboats, a dozen of them all at once. Aleck felt a new pang of anxiety stab through him: someone was using the Token of Time Dilation again. Waghalter became a blur, flames spitting from him in all directions, a dozen rifle-shots ringing out at once. Had Blood Eagle handed the Token off to Waghalter? The longboats veered almost simultaneously, burning, masts broken, and then one by one fell to earth.

Light from the Wargus-Fire burned brighter. Now Digglies and Deep Ones started to gather, carrying sticks and knives, many of them splashed with blood. They poured into the front gates of the Circus.

Doomer rode up to Aleck and Beth. Akaz leapt out of his mouth and landed in front of them.

"Wow," said Doomer. "That was intense."

"Thanks, bub!" Akaz said.

"Thank *you*, man!" Doomer playfully saluted Aleck and Beth, "Motherfuckin' Woads!" and rode back into the crowd, forcing his way through toward the gates.

"Isn't this fantastic?" beamed Akaz.

"This is at *least* as bad as when I was a kid," said Aleck. "Your Givers are eating the entire city."

"Oh come on," said Akaz, angrily. "Hardly the *entire* city."

"If I could kill you, Akaz..." Aleck said through clenched teeth.

"Ingrate!" said Akaz.

"You manipulative son of a bitch! What the hell do I have to be grateful for? This bullshit," he flung his hand toward the Circus, "it's worse than my worst nightmare, you fucking piece of shit!"

He spat in Akaz's face.

"Whoa," said Beth. "Baby, he's our way home."

Akaz tensed, frowning deeply. Aleck's spit sizzled away to nothing.

"Fuck you! You're worse than Apraxos!" Aleck spat in Akaz's face again. Instant saliva-steam wafted away.

Akaz growled, a deep rumble that seemed to originate underground and resonate in his barrel-chest.

"Down," said Beth. Akaz audibly ground his teeth but did not move. "Now," she said. Akaz's forelegs flew out from under him and he fell to the ground. He frowned up at her, then at Aleck. Aleck looked down at him, seething. "Calm down, baby," Beth said quietly, her hand on his arm. She turned to Akaz. "You too."

"May I go," said Akaz, inflecting the question as a statement. Beth nodded. Akaz ran off into the city.

"Where you going?" she asked. He didn't respond. "I guess you hurt his feelings," she said to Aleck.

Aleck slumped on his undersized bicycle, sobbing, tears streaming down his face.

Beth put her arms around him. "Give it up, baby. You've got to give it up. We failed. There was probably no way for us to succeed. We had no plan. We had no time. Let it go." Sobs wracked Aleck's body. "You've held onto this thing your whole life. And now you can let it go. You've got to. You gave it a go, and it went the way it went. Time to start a new life, based on now, you and me, not based on what happened when you were a kid." The battle continued raging inside the Circus of Burnt Skulls. The Herax chant had begun again, despite their lessening numbers: *We come as one! We come as one!*

After a while, Aleck's sobs died out. Beth wiped his face. "Want to go home?"

Aleck shook his head. "Let's go in."

"Come on, baby, it's too dangerous."

"Looks like it's almost over."

"What's the point, then? Maybe we could still make some kind of difference, but I'm not willing to just dive into a battlefield with you for kicks or guilt. You need to stop blaming yourself for all this, for once and for all."

Aleck looked down and shook his head.

"You were better off blaming Akaz."

Aleck looked at her. "I want to talk to Waghalter. Maybe when the Herax retreat back to the Herax Zone he can go around making sure there's no more massacres."

Beth took a deep breath. "So we go in there and hide, till we get a nice, safe opening to talk to him?"

"Sure. And I want to talk to my younger self."

"You're pushin' it. That's just the kind of thing to attract the Patrol's attention. And do you really want to lay your guilt trip on him? Do you really feel it's done you any good, living with that on your shoulders?"

"Maybe not." Aleck stared at the ground. "Maybe not."

"Come on," said Beth. They rode across the plaza, merging with the cheering crowd, and walked their bikes inside. In the tunnel bodies jostled them roughly, and they cursed as they bumped their knees and shins against their pedals.

Inside the Circus burned an enormous fire of wrecked Herax ships mingled with trees. Around the giant bonfire danced hundreds upon hundreds of Givers, Wilders, Digglies, and Deep Ones, under the swarm of chanting Herax. Beth pulled Aleck toward an overhang beside the gates. "This looks safe-ish." They stood astride their bicycles, watching the battle. After a few minutes they saw Waghalter's van land its raft a hundred yards away.

"Come on," said Aleck. "Now's our chance."

"Not yet." Beth held him back. "It's way too crazy out there." As if in response, a longboat swooped low toward the van, Herax hurling volley after volley of javelins. Waghalter shot it out of the air and it fell to the arena floor, crushing a wide, bloody swath through the crowd.

Waghalter jumped down from the van. "Jack!" said Aleck, but Waghalter didn't hear, and vanished into the crowd. A few moments later, they saw the motorcycle speed away, Waghalter on the back with his rifle, his red-haired wife driving it. The van lifted back into the air, Doomer manning the machine gun.

Most of the time the thinning swarm of the Herax fleet hovered far out of reach, sending down single boats like tentative feelers to attack the periphery far from Waghalter's van or concentrations of fire-throwing Givers. Occasionally, a shocking number of boats and ships dove low at once, a vast wave in frighteningly complex formations, hundreds of Herax chanting *We come as one!*—each time leaving fallen ships in the stands or upon the Wargus-Fire.

A burning thirty-foot sapling flew end over end through the air and crashed into the mast of a diving longboat. The boat flipped over, dumping its crew onto the fire, then falling on them. The crowd roared with joy.

"Wait, I remember that," said Aleck. "Waghalter threw that tree."

"What?" asked Beth. "How?"

"He must be possessed by Akaz, super-strong. He's standing in the fire."

"But Akaz just went that way." Beth pointed toward the gate.

"Not our Akaz," said Aleck, "the Waghalters' Akaz."

Jack and Beth Waghalter rode past on the motorcycle.

"Hey!" Aleck called after them.

Beth grabbed his robe. "Let's go home. You've got books to write and songs to record. *That's* what your life's for, not to obsess about this shitty little battle on this shitty little world."

Young Aleck, running after the Waghalters, skidded to a stop in front of Aleck and Beth. "What the hell!" he said, staring at them.

Akaz ran up to them. "There you are! Look," he said to Beth, "help me convince this kid to get out of here and lay low. He's jeopardizing everything we've done."

"You fuck!" Aleck shouted at Akaz. "You crawling fucking chaos!"

"Duh," said Akaz. "What did you expect, a tea party? This is war."

Aleck dismounted his bicycle and let it fall clattering onto its side. "Damn you, Akaz, you said our Cannibal-King would be a 'master of moral restraint'! Those were your exact words!"

"Look. Tomorrow I'll argue would'ves and could'ves with you all damn day. For now, just get your younger self out of here!"

"To hell with you!" Aleck turned to Young Aleck. "Hey kid, do me a favor, go get javelined or something."

"Aleck!" said Beth.

"Sorry." Aleck turned to her. "What the fuck are we supposed to do?" He looked around at the crowd and the fire.

"Look around you!" said Akaz. "Melkhaios is free!"

"*You* look!" Aleck pointed at Shallow Ones hung on hooks, a pile of Normals being pounded with sticks. "Look!" he pointed to struggling prisoners being flung onto the fire. Creatures prowling the Wargus-Fire devoured burning bodies. "You're nothing but crawling chaos, and this is nothing but a gigantic Rite of Augermath! And you tricked me into helping you!" He turned to Young Aleck. "Look, man, I remember this from when I was your age."

"Aleck, leave him alone," said Beth.

"Just get him out of here," said Akaz.

"Just imagine," Aleck said to his younger self, offering Beth a mollifying glance. "What if you could go back in time, and change the past."

"Aleck!" said Beth.

"Change what?" asked Young Aleck.

"What?" asked Aleck.

"What the fuck would I want to change?" asked Young Aleck.

Aleck furrowed his brow. "The killing innocent people part."

"Whatever, pussy." Young Aleck spat on the ground. "Those people are fucking assholes, fuck them."

Aleck looked at him, stunned. "That's not me," he said to Akaz, pointing at Young Aleck.

"Whatever, bitch," said Young Aleck. "Who'd wanna be you anyway, you old fuckface? All I want is to get my hands on them kick-ass Cannibal-King guns of his."

"Look, will you please get him out of here?" asked Akaz.

"What difference does it make?" asked Aleck.

"What?" asked Akaz.

"He's not me. If something happens to him, it won't affect my past."

"Wrong, damn it, there's still resonances!" said Akaz. "He dies here, chances are your actual younger self gets run over by a truck back on your Earth or some goddamn weird-lucky bullshit like that!" He turned to Young Aleck. "Come on, kid, I'll get you drunk, then we'll get you back home the way you came."

"Whatever, bitch," said this Young Aleck of some obnoxious parallel Earth. "Get it? Bitch means a female dog. I called you a girl."

"I'm coming around on this javelin idea," said Beth.

"It's embarrassing," said Aleck. "My cognate, the insufferable prick."

"Look, kid!" said Akaz. "Get the hell away from here, before you summon the Reality Patrol! Beth, get him out of here!"

"Why me?" said Beth. "I don't even want to deal with his foul little mouth."

"I'll deal with your mouth, biotch," said Young Aleck. "A-ny-time."

Beth's grabbed Young Aleck by the hair. "C'mere," she said.

He tore away from her and grabbed the pink bicycle from the ground, swinging it around in a wide swipe toward her, Aleck, and Akaz. Then he hopped on with it already rolling. "Fuck all y'all!" he said, standing up on the pedals, diving into the crowd.

They chased him. Aleck fell behind first, then Beth. Akaz disappeared in the mass of people. Aleck caught up to Beth. "What now?" she asked.

"That little asshole is going to fuck this up worse than it already is!" Aleck panted, pointing angrily after Young Aleck.

"I want to smack the mouth off of his face. But I'd rather just get the hell out of here and go home."

"Come on. Let's just try to get him out of here, like Akaz asked us."

"That little prick is not you. I honestly do not give a shit what happens to him."

"You heard Akaz, though. Resonances. If something happens to him, I could get hit by a truck. Let me on there with you."

Beth fumed for a moment, then stood up on the pedals. Aleck balanced on the seat as she drove them into the crowd. They proceeded with difficulty, locals gawking at the bicycle in spite of the enchantment of their Keeper robes.

Eventually they entered the mouth of a dark tunnel. Burning debris lit the far gate. Once in the street, they realized this was not the way they had come: the garish shops *Giver Drums* and *Real Giver Drums* were nowhere to be seen. A block away lay an ornate Herax ship, half smashed, debris and bodies scattered around it. Beth and Aleck rode past a fallen pink bicycle, Young Aleck's Adidas sneaker tangled in the gear.

Near the shipwreck, Jack and Beth Waghalter stood to either side of their motorcycle. Behind them, Akaz backed away, looking nervous. Young Aleck stood beside Jack, pestering him, while Beth fired her pistol into the distance. Jack seemed to be trying to keep his rifle away from Young Aleck. Black wolf-jaws—another Akaz—sprouted from Jack's mouth to snarl, "Get away from us, kid!"

Aleck and Beth rode up. Aleck got a good look at Beth Waghalter's freckled face; for a white woman, her features were shaped startlingly like those of his own wife. His eyes met hers.

"Aleck," said Beth, "this is bad."

"Roger. Let's get the fuck out of here." Aleck slid off so Beth could turn the bike, then hopped back on.

Akaz looked back over his shoulder to see them teetering on the rickety bicycle. "No, no, no, you jackasses," he said as he backed quickly away from both Waghalters and Woads, "get the hell out of here, *now!*"

Beth stood up on the pedals.

"We are!" said Aleck.

"Freeze!" blasted an electronically amplified voice. "Reality Patrol!" A dozen Reality Patrol special operatives appeared in a circle around them, most of them aiming tempochromed weapons.

"Oh no," said Aleck and Beth together. They pulled their hoods and robes tightly around themselves, holding each other close.

The techs recited readings from their omnometers. "Two temporal recursions," said one of them. "One entirely foreign, one mixed."

*Two me's and two Akazes*, thought Aleck.

"Two entirely foreign parallel recursions—" said another technician.

*The Woads and the Waghalters.*

"—With a local-slash-mixed trine parallel," continued the tech, "— correction, that's quincunx—hold on, I'm registering an error...."

"Get ready to dodge," said Aleck.

"I loved our life," said Beth.

They stared into each other's eyes.

"I'm registering an error as well," said a third tech. "It's off my scale; filtering for ECSS.... Oh my God! *They all have Weird Luck!*"

"Hold your fire!" blasted the captain's voice. Then, a burst of static, and "—fire!"

*Aleck tried to dodge aside, but a beam hit him square in the back. He fell over, taking Beth and the bicycle with him. He heard her whisper his name. Please god, he thought, don't let me die on this world....*

# Epilogue on Denebola Base

Aleck found himself floating, surrounded by featureless whiteness.

Not floating. Lying on a floor. Smooth; firm but spongy.

He crawled around the room, numb, foggy-headed. Definitely drugged. He found a wall. Pulled himself upright. With a little effort he confirmed he was in a featureless eight-foot cube. A padded cell.

Suddenly acutely conscious of Beth's absence, he felt grateful for the mind-numbing drugs.

He took a piss in the corner. The floor absorbed it.

Aleck sat for a long time, trying to think.

A flash of light and Clark appeared. Not Clark: a low-res holographic image of him.

"Clark," said Aleck.

"I'm nearly Acting Archivist now," buzzed Clark's voice. "I thought you should know."

"Says who, your boss at the Reality Patrol?"

"So decrees Great Thoth," said Clark. "I need but one thing from you."

Aleck felt a twinge through the fogginess.

"Where's Beth," he asked.

Clark smiled at him.

"Where's Beth!"

"Where," asked Clark, "is the Fifth Key to the Archive?"

Aleck stared at him.

Clark smiled.

*— Oakland, Calif.; North Hollywood, Calif.*
*Jan. 1, 2004 – Dec. 12, 2005*